SECRET LETTERS
FROM 0 to 10

SECRET LETTERS
FROM 0 to 10

by Susie Morgenstern

translated by Gill Rosner

VIKING

VIKING
Published by the Penguin Group
Penguin Putnam Books for Young Readers, 345 Hudson Street,
New York, New York 10014, U.S.A.
Penguin Books Ltd, 27 Wrights Lane, London W8 5TZ, England
Penguin Books Australia Ltd, Ringwood, Victoria, Australia
Penguin Books Canada Ltd, 10 Alcorn Avenue, Toronto, Ontario, Canada M4V 3B2
Penguin Books (N..Z.) Ltd, 182–192 Wairau Road, Auckland 10, New Zealand
Penguin Books Ltd, Registered Offices: Harmondsworth, Middlesex, England

First published in 1996 in France under the title *Lettres d'amour de 0 á 10*
by l'école des loisirs.
Published in 1998 in the United States of America by Viking, a member
of Penguin Putnam Books for Young Readers.
1   3   5   7   9   10   8   6   4   2

LIBRARY OF CONGRESS CATALOGING-IN-PUBLICATION DATA
Morgenstern, Susie Hoch.
[Lettres d'amour de 0 à 10. English]
Secret letters from 0 to 10 / by Susie Morgenstern ; translated by Gill Rosner.
p.   cm.
Summary: Ten-year-old Ernest lives a boring existence in Paris with his grandmother
until a lively girl named Victoria enters his class at school.
ISBN 0-670-88007-8
[1. Friendship—Fiction.   2. Schools—Fiction.   3. Paris (France)]
PZ7.M826714Sg   [Fic]—dc21   1998   98-5559   CIP   AC

Printed in U.S.A.
Set in Garamond

For Philippe Silvy

Ernest

He always walked slowly toward the building where he lived, never raising his head, always taking the same old way. It had never entered his mind to try the slightest variation in his route. He had never even crossed to the other side of the street. He would just take himself straight to school, then straight back home again.

Every day he trudged up the same fifty-seven steps to the third floor. He never skipped steps or rushed. Ernest was never in a hurry. The ten years of his life had passed so far at a turtle's pace, as if it had been slowed down by the premature onset of old age.

Every day he put his schoolbag down in his room which, although the smallest, was the least cluttered in the house. It could have been a closet or a cell in an old prison: just a bed, a table, a chair, and a closet, all in immaculate order. He took out his schoolbooks and got ready for his homework before going to get his snack from the kitchen table.

A large green apple and a cracker had been waiting there for him since lunchtime. Every day, the housekeeper put them out after clearing away his lunch. The snack was always the same.

After a few bites he usually didn't feel like any more of the apple, but he finished it just the same. Then he began to do his homework, working methodically and with concentration. He knew that the quicker it was done, the sooner he would be free to take another look inside the only cupboard in the house which was not kept locked.

When his grandmother heard the creak of the book cabinet door, the chinking of its fine glass pane, she left her room and came to sit down with Ernest in the living room while he read.

"Good evening, Grandmother," said Ernest, joining her on the shabby velvet couch. No one had ever called her by her first name: Precious. It was hard to imagine anyone calling her that.

Grandmother tilted her head in greeting. She spoke rarely and little. Ernest always had the impression that if she moved too much, she would disintegrate. She was eighty years old, but the kind of eighty that is really old, like the grandmothers in fairy tales. Her skin was so wrinkled and crinkled and dry that Ernest was afraid if ever she happened to smile, it would turn to dust. But she never did smile. She walked with difficulty and ate without appetite. She looked after her grandson out of a sense of duty. She was all he had.

She had brought Ernest up since his mother had died when he was born. In the Morlaisse family, people died from history's little accidents: the Second World War had claimed his grandfather, the First World War his great grandfather, and as for his father, he had disappeared: an unexplained disappearance after his wife's funeral, when Ernest was just one day old.

And so his grandmother had lost her own father when she was five and her husband when she was thirty, and when she lost her son at seventy, she had inherited a baby for whom she had neither the physical nor the moral strength. But she did what she saw had to be done.

She had instantly hired a woman hardly younger than herself to look after the baby's hygiene and nutrition. This woman, Germaine, had at that time just lost her husband. She had no children, and was looking more for an escape from loneliness than a salary. The two women got along well, because they had their principles in common . . . a lot of principles. They lived side by side in a parallel existence. Madame Morlaisse had offered to let Germaine live there, but Germaine preferred to come and go, except at the very beginning when the baby wasn't sleeping through the night yet, or sometimes if the weather was very bad.

Although Germaine was old, too, she tried to disguise her age with all the techniques of modern makeup. In fact, her creams and lotions were the only signs of the modern world in this machineless, televisionless house. Germaine struggled constantly against gray hair, wrinkles, and fat; however she had given up on the fight against depression. During his first years, she had spoken the only words Ernest ever heard, but as soon as he started school, she had clammed up like her employer.

Any conversation was limited to the strictly utilitarian, and even this was hardly necessary, for the house ran itself, apparently from sheer force of habit and lassitude; it seemed to be in a permanent state of regulated minimum service.

Germaine did the shopping and the cooking. She could have ordered the groceries by telephone, but there was no telephone. Another woman, a friend of hers, and just as old, did the housework. All their laundry was sent out.

Madame Morlaisse just sat, a silent mournful statue. At one time, she used to read beside Ernest, but now her eyes tired too easily. Often, Ernest would raise his head from his book and notice that Grandmother was dozing off, still sitting upright in her chair. Sometimes she even managed to snore, which added an extra sound effect to the usual tick tock of the clocks. Ernest knew that Grandmother wouldn't have liked to know that she snored, so he never said a word.

Even if she was in a deep sleep, she would suddenly rouse herself to listen to the eight o'clock news. The radio was one of the first models ever made, and getting her station was like trying to listen to the radio from London during the war, with the same faint sound and

5

loud crackling. Madame Morlaisse was becoming rather hard of hearing, and it wasn't part of the newscaster's job to repeat everything three times just for her benefit. However, this was of no importance. Mrs. Morlaisse didn't really want to know what was happening in the world. From time to time she would react to certain words, names, or countries. If the newscaster happened to say Germany for example, she would repeat with a sigh, "Germany."

The important thing for her was to switch on the radio at eight o'clock, exactly as she had done every evening for all these years.

For his part, Ernest listened to the news with rapt attention from beginning to end. It was as if he half expected to hear the answer he was looking for. He wasn't interested in politics, politicians, or elections. What he was listening for, from his place on the sofa, was news of the outbreak of the Third World War, for, like those which had come before, it was sure to carry off yet another Morlaisse.

At 8:30 the Morlaisses had supper. The menu was always the same: soup. Soup is easy to digest, it makes you grow, and it guarantees a good night's sleep—that is, if it is salt- and pepper-free, of course. Germaine didn't come back in the evenings. Ernest would heat up the soup and then, having put the dirty dishes into the sink, he would go quietly to bed. Regular sleep is important for a child. Before brushing his teeth, he always said, "Goodnight, Grandmother, sleep well." Her eyes would blink in reply.

Thus, Ernest got up every weekday morning with the regularity of a well-oiled machine. He would eat two pieces of toast with marmalade (made by a cousin of Germaine's in the south of France), drink a glass of warm milk, put on his tie, pack his schoolbag, and go to school. Every day he came home for lunch, because both Germaine and his grandmother were suspicious of school food. To them, something canned or frozen wasn't food. And fish did not come in fingers, but with scales and heads. Potatoes arrived caked with mud, straight from the soil, without stopping at a processing plant. Madame Morlaisse was wary of too much salt, too much sugar, and bad influences in general. Germaine was suspicious of oil that might be rancid, fried food, rotten meat, and too much noise.

Ernest owned neither jeans nor a sweatsuit. Twice a year, a tailor would come to the house, take his measurements, and make him a suit too old-fashioned for this century and too modern for the last. It looked like something that might have been part of a school uniform. The same tailor supplied his shirts, ties, handkerchiefs, underwear, and socks, and his annual winter coat.

This getup kept the other children far away from Ernest, as if he had something contagious. In any case, he would have avoided them—not because he wanted to but because it was the safe thing to do.

Nobody made fun of him—everybody was used to him. And he was by far the top of the class, except in composition when the subject was "My favorite TV Show," "My Vacation," or "My Sunday."

Ernest's Sundays were even less eventful than the other days of the week. The minutes clogged past like sand in a wet egg-timer. Germaine only came on Sundays to cook and serve lunch—a Sunday lunch with meat, two vegetables, and stewed fruit for dessert.

After her nap, Madame Morlaisse would call Ernest into the living room, and, taking out a key from against her withered chest, she would open the door of the inlaid cabinet and extract a narrow china box which was the repository of *the letter.* She and Ernest would sit at the table that rested on a pedestal the shape of a golden lion.

"Will you read it, Grandmother?" Ernest would ask.

Madame Morlaisse would extract the sheet of paper from its envelope, carefully unfold it, and stare at it as if it contained the key to all the secrets of the universe. The only problem was, the letter was illegible. Even though Ernest knew this, every Sunday he would hope against hope. He might be at the top of the class, but he couldn't figure out even one of the letters. There were no *a*'s, *b*'s, or even *z*'s. There was just a jungle of knots shouting their message inaudibly from the page.

His great-grandfather had sent this letter from a village near the front during World War I. Of all the secrets in the house, this one was the biggest—or possibly the second biggest. Ernest hoped that if he continued to do well in school, one day he would be able to decipher all the secrets.

Victoria

Ernest was not the smiling type. At school, he spoke only if spoken to. His answers were always thoughtful and correct, and his comments sensible and intelligent. Ernest liked school, because the soothing music of other people's chatter made him feel less alone; he also hoped that school might hold the key which would one day enable him to unlock the secret scrawled on the faded page of the letter.

The boys at school always left him to his solitude.

The girls, on the other hand, did everything to try to attract his attention, to enter into his world and capture him with their warmth and their laughter. One thing that Ernest could never hide was the fact that he was handsome. All the girls dreamed of getting close enough to touch him, or at least to get him to look at them with those black eyes of his, which he only seemed to use for looking at the ground, the sky, or the pages of books.

On Ernest's desk, girls deposited cookies which would stay there until the cleaning lady cleared them away. Ernest was not impolite, he had simply never eaten a cookie, and he was afraid to try one. Germaine and Precious didn't eat them. Sometimes he'd find candy, or exotic fruit on his desk, but he knew that the rules didn't allow eating between meals.

Often notes would come his way. He never even thought of opening them, so he had no idea of the messages inside: "Ernest, I love you." "You're gorgeous; I made this cake for you." "Please come to my party on Wednesday." Love notes full of hopeless hope.

At recess, Ernest sat on a bench reading. After class, he went straight home. He never looked right or left. Some of the girls would follow him, dreaming that he might notice them and say something. They knew where he lived, and would wait there, hoping for a hello that never came.

Ernest's routine life had no rough edges. Each day

was an infallible repetition of the last. There were no surprises . . . that is, until one Monday at the beginning of November. The principal barged into the classroom, pushing a new girl in front of her. "I want you all to meet Victoria de Montardent. From now on, she'll be in your class."

Ernest was a bit surprised. This Victoria girl was different from the others. She was dressed a little like he was: navy-blue blazer over a pleated skirt, and a white shirt. Her long black hair was held back by a black headband. Since the half of the desk next to him was the only one free, the teacher told her to sit there. She sat down and without any hesitation greeted him with a cheery, "Hi there!" He had no choice but to return it.

When the teacher handed a book to his new neighbor, Ernest showed her the right page. He could hardly do otherwise—as the teacher kept saying, "Ernest, I'm counting on you to explain everything to Victoria."

Ernest did as he was asked, like a robot, without looking at Victoria but making sure she understood by murmuring, "Do you see?" to which the reply was an emphatic, "Sure do, thanks to you."

At recess, instead of hanging around with the other girls, she followed Ernest to his bench, and read like he did—except that since she had no book of her own, she sat next to him and read his, making herself keep up, so as to be ready when he turned the page.

After the break, Ernest shut his book and went back to the classroom, with Victoria tagging along. At lunchtime, Ernest put on his coat, and Victoria trailed behind him all the way home. When he opened his front door, she shouted, "I live a little further on. I'll pick you up on the way back. Have a great lunch!"

When he came out of the house, she was waiting for him. Ernest strode along, as if Victoria did not exist. To stop him from ignoring her, she grabbed his arm and asked, "Have you lived here for long?" Ernest nodded. "Don't you ever have lunch at school?" He shook his head. "Have you got any brothers and sisters?" He shook his head again. "Are your parents strict?" It didn't matter whether Ernest answered or not—Victoria had enough conversation for both of them. "My parents are really strict. We can't even watch TV till we've done our homework. What's your favorite show? What's your favorite food? Who's your favorite singer? What do you do after school? I have piano lessons and swimming. Where do you go for vacation? Have you got a collection? I collect the aluminum foil from chocolate bars.

Have you ever been to a foreign country? Do your parents let you go to parties?"

For someone who was at the top of the class, Ernest was very stupid about answering all these questions. He couldn't answer a single one. He didn't know the names of any singers or TV shows. As for his favorite food, he had never thought about it—the rule was "you eat what is put in front of you." Maybe he should say it was soup, seeing as how that was what he ate most often. But in fact, he didn't particularly care for soup. As for a collection, the only thing he could think of were the fifty-seven stairs up to his apartment, or the number of steps he took on his way to school (he had often counted them). Or the number of minutes which ticked their way through the day without anyone noticing, or those other minutes which dragged along so slowly they made you feel like you were sleepwalking.

"I've asked enough questions for the moment. Don't you have any for me?"

Ernest was worried. Nobody had ever questioned him and he hadn't learned how to do it to other people. Anyway, curiosity about other people wasn't really his strong point. Nevertheless, he tried. He scouted around in as-yet unused corners of his brain trying to discover the tiniest hint of an interrogative. But nothing came as far as his mouth. It wasn't fair, when for once, he really did want to talk to somebody. As if she understood his predicament, she said, "Don't worry, Ernest. You're so good looking, you don't need to say anything to make yourself more interesting." She was still hanging onto his arm. Ernest couldn't believe his ears. Good looking. Him? This was the first he had heard about it.

A question . . . any question. You shouldn't ask a question if you don't want to know the answer. He turned toward her suddenly and began with a stammer, "Um . . . Victoria! Um . . . Why did they name you Victoria?"

He was expecting a history lesson on some British queen, but she answered, "Because I was born after they had had twelve boys. My parents wanted a girl so much that they tried thirteen times . . . and finally they had me. My name means 'victory.'"

Ernest wondered if the twelfth boy had been named Defeat. "Twelve brothers!" he sighed.

"Well, now there are thirteen. My mother wanted to try one last time for another girl, but it didn't work. It was a boy. He's six months old."

"It's like an army," thought Ernest. All afternoon he couldn't stop thinking about Victoria, surrounded by those thirteen boys. It stopped him from concentrating, but he was so well trained that his work more or less did itself. Victoria still followed him around. At break, she read over his shoulder again. The other girls in the class hung around them in a circle of discontent, but "the couple" didn't seem to notice.

When, at the end of the day, the teacher handed Victoria a pile of worn-out schoolbooks, telling her to cover them by the next day, she plunked half of them right into Ernest's arms and demanded, "You don't mind walking me home, do you?"

Jeremy

As they approached his block, Ernest wanted to drop the books and tell Victoria, "I'm afraid I can't go any farther." But the pile was really too heavy for one person, and he had enough common sense to realize that you can't let a fellow human being down in a moment of need. Nevertheless, going outside his own tiny neighborhood gave him the creeps. Not that his grandmother had ever forbidden it, but it just felt weird. He was amazed, once they had passed his block, to find that he was still breathing and no lightning had struck him down. His grandmother had never punished him; there had never been any reason to.

Ernest was amazed at what he was seeing. No more than three hundred yards from the house which had held him prisoner for ten years, the sight of dogs, children, and other living creatures all running free suddenly made his heart beat faster. For the first time ever, he felt daring, like an urban hunter, an explorer in his own neighborhood, almost a hero.

He followed Victoria across a garden square as far as the entrance to her building, which was just opposite all this greenery. He set the books down in front of the gate, saying, "Okay, all set." This "Okay, all set" summed up Ernest's feelings of having completed his responsibilities: "I have done my duty as a neighbor and classmate, my duty as a citizen, as a human being."

"Ready to head upstairs?" Victoria promptly thrust her pile of books into Ernest's arms, bent down to pick up the pile he had put down, and pushed her reluctant porter toward the elevator. The pile of books shook, betraying Ernest's nervousness.

"I'll walk up," Ernest said.

"Are you crazy? It's on the seventh floor. Seventh heaven my dad calls it." And she tucked him neatly into the cast-iron cage which slowly hiccupped its way upward.

Ernest held his breath. "Are children allowed to take the elevator?"

Victoria raised an eyebrow and closed one eye in order to think about this. "Why not?"

Miraculously still alive when they got out of the elevator, Ernest, with another "Okay, all set!" dumped the books down in front of the only door in the hallway. But before he had the chance to rush down the stairs, the front door opened, revealing a stocky young man with a baby in his arms. The baby, smiling and gurgling, held out its chubby arms toward Ernest, who was glued to the spot, petrified.

"Take him, he wants you," ordered Victoria. "This is Jeremy."

Jeremy reached out and began clinging to Ernest like a leech. Ernest was now certain that lightning had finally struck. How could he be holding a baby? This was impossible. But just then, he felt something funny. He felt a smile come across his face, stretching his mouth from ear to ear. Jeremy held him tight between his two chubby arms, almost suffocating him. Ernest had never been hugged before in his life. This truly was seventh heaven.

"Don't stand out there! Come in!" said the young man.

"I can't. I have to go," and he murmured a feeble good-bye as he headed down the stairs.

"Ernest, you're taking the baby with you!" Victoria shouted after him.

"Oh sorry! I didn't realize," said Ernest, coming back up the stairs.

"Well, you know, one more or one less . . ."

"There. He's all yours," declared Ernest, trying to detach the baby, who was holding on for dear life.

"Come on in," repeated the stocky young man.

"That's my big brother, Dan, he's twenty-two. Dan, this is Ernest, my best friend."

Ernest was struck by the word "friend." He followed them into the hallway, which was piled high with big cardboard boxes, then along a corridor designed principally, it seemed, for roller-skating in and out of more cartons. Three roller skaters were in the middle of a championship match. "That's Zebulun, Naphtali, and Asher," whispered Victoria. "They're real pests."

These three seemed to be nearer his age. Ernest wondered if the names were African. He repeated them out loud. "Zebulun, Naphtali, Asher?"

"My parents wanted a set of names that went together. They thought of all the kings of France, but they couldn't name all their sons Louis. They knew they wanted a lot of children, so they decided to start off with the twelve tribes of Israel."

"You mean the ones in the Bible?"

"Yes, you know them?"

"There's an old Bible at home. I've looked through it, but I don't remember all the names."

They reached a huge living room, where four other tribes were fighting over the remote control. The TV, the only object which had been unpacked, was on full blast, and so were they.

"That's Gad, Benjamin, Joseph, and Levi."

The baby was still in Ernest's arms, when he felt a warm liquid trickle down his hand and gush onto the floor like Niagara Falls. Victoria spotted it at once, and scolded Dan. "Have you changed him in the last century, or what?"

"I just got here. Ask Judah. He was on duty."

"Forget it! We'll do it ourselves."

Victoria asked Ernest to follow her into the room she shared with Jeremy at the other end of the huge apartment. The room was a zoo full of stuffed animals, mobiles, music boxes, and toys, all spilling out of empty cartons. Ernest thought of his own cell-like room and wondered how Victoria managed to do homework in such a mess.

He put Jeremy down as Victoria told him to, on a plastic covered board, and watched her go about her duties with an experienced hand, like a miniature mother. Once she had finished Jeremy, she started on Ernest. Leaving the baby propped up against a giant teddy bear, she took Ernest by the hand and led him to the kitchen.

The apartment was in proportion to the family, full of doors which looked like they might lead into a thousand and one rooms. Near one of these, Victoria pointed to another brother sitting at his desk. "That's Reuben. He spends his life doing homework. He's off baby duty for this year because of his exams."

In the kitchen, Issachar and Simeon were peeling a ton of potatoes. It seemed that a whole regiment lived on this floor, although Ernest hadn't actually counted them. "Open your mouth," demanded Victoria, and thrust at him what looked like a flat dark brown square of rubber.

That did it. Ernest could obey no longer. "I really have to go now!"

"Have some chocolate first."

"No thanks, really."

"But you have to help me. If you eat half the bar, I'll have my thousandth aluminum foil wrapper for my collection. Just taste it! It's pure bitter chocolate."

"No, really, my snack is waiting for me at home." Ernest backed away, saying, "Good-bye." He heard the abandoned Jeremy screaming in the other room. "The baby's crying," he informed them in the kitchen.

"Don't worry, it's his only means of self-expression. We all went through that once," Victoria said as she showed him to the door. But there was one thing Ernest had to know before he left.

"Victoria, tell me, do you have parents?"

She raised an eyebrow and closed one eye. "Ernest! What a question! Of course I do, everyone has parents! You've got them, don't you?"

"Well, actually, no, I don't," said Ernest, as he fled.

Precious

Ernest looked thoughtfully at the elevator which could take him effortlessly to the third floor. In spite of a sudden wave of exhaustion, force of habit took him to the staircase. As he went up the fifty-seven steps, his head felt strangely separate from the rest of his body. He kept seeing the baby, Victoria, the horde of boys, and he wondered how it was possible for one woman to have had so many children while another died giving birth to just one.

Fourteen children! That meant that Victoria's mother had spent ten and a half years being pregnant, and at least fifty-six months being very fat. And that was not all. Ernest considered the awful contents of Jeremy's diapers multiplied by fourteen. How did you clothe, feed, and bring up that number of children? And on top of that, the parents weren't even at home to see what was going on. "They work," Victoria had said. Of course, they had to, although as far as Ernest could see, all they ate in that house was potatoes.

Ernest went into the apartment, put his schoolbag in his room, glanced at the apple and the cracker waiting patiently for him, and took a detour in front of his grandmother's room. Everything was as usual. She hadn't realized that he was late, but he was honest. He whispered, not wanting to wake her, "I'm home, Grandmother. I was held up." Then he took another detour—it was a day for detours—into the living room, where the box with the letter in it waited to tantalize him. In a flash of inspiration Ernest realized, "Now all of a sudden I know fourteen people—well thirteen anyway—who can help me decipher the letter." For the second time in one day, he found himself smiling.

He bit hungrily into his apple and did his homework in record time, but when the moment came for his usual break, his eyes seemed stuck to the pages of his book. He couldn't manage to follow the lines, and the inexplicable alchemy which transforms symbols on paper into emotions in the heart no longer worked. The words seemed leaden and would not rise to filter through his brain. The sentences stagnated. He tried reading and rereading them, but his head was too full of the day's events.

Here and there, a word in his book would bring back what had happened, words like "brother" or "friend" which up to now had never had any particular effect on him. It was when he came across the word "invade" that he had the idea that Victoria had somehow invaded him. She had captured him, enslaved him, and she hadn't even asked him first. A dictator no less! Do or die! And Ernest, who could no longer stop himself, smiled for the third time. "Long live the bossy!"

By eight o'clock Grandmother had still not appeared in the living room. Ernest was alarmed. Maybe this was the lightning bolt he'd been afraid of? What if she was dead? He had to go see. It took him a few seconds to get up the courage to knock on her door, and a whole minute before going in. Grandmother was sitting on the bed, her feet touching the floor, and in her hand was an envelope. Seeing Ernest seemed to startle her. She immediately tried to hide the envelope under her pillow in a whole pile of letters.

"Grandmother, it's eight o'clock."

His grandmother nodded her head, rose to her feet, and started moving slowly. When she got to the living room, she turned on the radio, which, as always, spat out its dose of earthquakes, forest fires, famines, and civil wars. She turned it off and they went into the kitchen, where Ernest heated up the soup. For the first time in his life, he felt like telling her how he had spent his day.

She had never asked him. For them, days came and went and time passed as it must. You do what you have to do, and that's all there is to it, he'd always thought. Suddenly Ernest wanted there to be more. Once in a while, Ernest began thinking, maybe you have to make things happen.

"Grandmother," he said, without really knowing how he was going to tell her. (For her part, Precious found him a little agitated. The soup didn't seem to calm him down. "But he's grown. He's getting handsome," she thought. "He's looking more and more like his father." She sighed in a way which almost stopped Ernest from continuing.) There were so many things he wanted to ask her about or tell her, but he didn't know which to choose. He decided on the most harmless, although even it would bother her.

"Grandmother, today I didn't come straight home from school. I had to do a favor for a girl in my class. On the way to her house, we crossed a big garden square near here. Do you know it?"

She nodded her head.

"It's really beautiful, Grandmother." He paused for a moment. "Do you ever go out while I'm at school?"

She lowered her eyes, and murmured, "No." Ernest had already known that she never went out. And he felt guilty now about wanting her to. After all, he wasn't absolutely positive that going outside was good for your health. And he didn't know if his grandmother was in good health for someone so old. When she didn't feel well, she went to bed and slept. When Ernest had a cold, a sore throat, or an earache, she gave him aspirin. He had never missed school. She had never sent for the doctor. Illnesses passed . . . like the days.

That was it. He wanted to take his grandmother out. "I've never done anything for her," he thought. "And I know nothing about her." The image of her sitting motionless on the bed inspired him to follow through.

"Grandmother, what do you do all day?"

Precious looked at her grandson as if she had a bone stuck in her throat, as if something had disrupted their code of silence. Indeed, they had never talked much, and the words had been so thoroughly buried, pressed down, and squashed up inside her, they were practically sealed up. If words stop flowing, they clog up, freeze, and can no longer act as messengers of the soul.

"What do I do all day? I survive," she thought. To Ernest she said, "I do nothing. I rest."

"But Grandmother, taking a rest is for after you've done something." He remembered what his school-teacher had said: "Doing nothing makes you weak, sick, and crazy."

"I take a rest from life. I think about things."

"About what things, Grandmother?"

"About people who are dead."

This made Ernest unhappy. "The dead are dead, Grandmother. You can't bring them back."

"That's no reason to forget them."

"But you can remember them while you're doing something else, can't you?"

His grandmother seemed surprised by this idea.

He didn't want to go too far. It was, after all, thanks to

her that he had a roof over his head, that he was fed and clothed, that he had books to read . . . but he couldn't help blurting out, "Do you ever think about me?"

"I think more about those who are no longer with us. You are here. You leave in the morning, you come back, do your homework, you do nothing to upset me."

Regretfully Ernest thought to himself, "I do nothing to make you happy, either."

There was one thing he was burning to ask, but he dared not broach the subject. His grandmother had woken up a little. She was on the lookout and expecting another riddle. Ernest looked thoughtfully at the web that the spider of time had woven on her face, as if somehow these lines might reveal the answer to his question.

"Ernest, I think I'll have a little more soup," she said in order to prolong this moment. Ernest got up, puzzled by her unexpected appetite. He sat down again, leaned his elbows on the table, put his chin in his hands, and asked his question:

"Grandmother, is my father dead?"

Germaine

"Your father is not dead." His grandmother's words had rung in his head all night and kept him from sleeping. Ernest had not dared ask the other questions which haunted him: "Then where is he? Why doesn't he come to see me? Why doesn't he write?" These questions had remained unasked, clinging to his teeth as he brushed them, to the tangles in his hair, and lurking behind the eyes that looked at him in the mirror.

Germaine was quietly occupied in the kitchen, washing the two bowls from last night. Grandmother was sitting down for breakfast, and Ernest was just coming in with his usual good morning, when the doorbell, which had never been known to make a sound, suddenly rang out loud enough to waken the dead. This transformed the women from two pictures of composure into two gargoyles of utter panic.

"I'll get it," announced Germaine.

No sooner was the door opened, than Victoria bounded into the hallway and made her way toward the kitchen.

"Hi! I'm Victoria de Montardent, Ernest's girlfriend."

Germaine followed her the whole way, powerless to prevent this bulldozer from charging into the house.

Victoria dumped a bagful of croissants and rolls on the table. "My dad simply went wild at the bakery this morning. We couldn't eat it all, so I took a few and decided to come and eat them here with Ernest before school." Totally unaware of the effect she was having, Victoria went on. "How are you guys anyway? Did you have a good night, sweet dreams, and all that? I dreamed about Ernest. We were grown up and in love. We were about to get married, and then I don't know the rest because Jeremy woke up screaming. I think he was probably dreaming about you, too!"

Victoria didn't need any encouragement to go on with her story, but she had to stop to breathe, taking the opportunity to grab a big brioche, which she immediately put back into the bag.

"Help yourselves!" she ordered, handing round the bag. "It's rude to serve myself first. Mom says that all she can hope for is to bring us up without any major catastrophes. She knows that expecting us to have good manners would be asking too much."

Germaine and Precious sat frozen to their chairs in shock. Ernest, however, tried to do the right thing and took a croissant from the bag. He scrutinized it as if it had come from a factory on Mars, then, out of politeness, and without looking at the two wardens of his eating habits, he bravely crammed the crisp golden brown object into his mouth, fully expecting to die then and there.

"Hey, it's warm. It's delicious," he declared, using a word which until that moment he had known only in theory. "Try one, Grandmother, you'll see."

"I know what they are," came the abrupt reply.

"Try one, Germaine." Germaine did not want to give in, but she weakened at the sight of a huge chocolate-filled croissant. To assuage her guilt, she pushed the bag toward Precious saying, "Go on, eat it, just this once . . ."

"Have you got any hot chocolate?" asked Victoria.

"We have chicory coffee," replied Germaine with an air of superiority.

"Oh. Well in that case, I'll settle for a glass of cold milk."

"It's bad for the digestion," warned Germaine.

"But it makes you grow."

"Do you really want to grow so quickly, Mademoiselle?"

"Oh yes! Then I can marry Ernest!"

Ernest felt butterflies of pleasure in his stomach but at the same time, he felt more and more uneasy. His grandmother and Germaine were silent, but alert. It was as if a spark of curiosity, a spark of life itself, had finally lit up their tomb-like existence. A doorway seemed to have opened.

Ernest looked anxiously at the clock. "We have to go. It's late." He had always been able to take his time before. He didn't know what it was like to hurry.

"Okay. Off to the torture chamber!" cried Victoria. "By the way, don't expect Ernest home for lunch. He's coming to us. Mom's at home today and she wants to meet the man in my life. We're having beef fondue. I love it. I was the one who chose it. Then after school I'll come and do my homework here, because I'm not on baby duty today for a change. Okey-dokey? Let's go!" She rushed at Grandmother and Germaine, and kissed them both on their two flabby cheeks. Spurred by her enthusiasm, Ernest did likewise . . . for the first time in his life!

Ernest didn't walk at his usual pace. He didn't run, either. He just followed Victoria.

He couldn't see the envy of the other girls, who were getting ready to attack Victoria. But Victoria did see them. She read the anonymous notes on her desk: "We knew him before you! Watch out!" "Watch it, you cow. Leave Ernest alone!" "Traitor, witch, Ernest is ours."

She answered each note with the same patient explanation: "I love Ernest. That's all there is to it. We can't help it. And what is more, I understand him, and I want him to be happy. We're getting married in thirteen years, eight months, and three days. This is an invitation to our wedding."

As usual, Ernest worked above and beyond the call of duty. But now he really put his heart into it, since he had discovered that he had one. His sleepy old heart had begun to wake up, his grumpy old heart had begun to laugh, his silent old heart had begun making new sounds, his unquestioning old heart had begun to ask questions. From now on, his heart was attached by an almost visible thread to that of his neighbor, the victorious, imperious, impetuous, and hilarious Victoria.

He uttered no word of protest when she pushed him right past his building at lunchtime that day.

"Do you like beef fondue?"

"I don't know. I've never tried it."

"Do you like chili con carne?" Making gentle fun of him, she replied to her own question. "I don't know, I've never had any! Don't worry, Ernest, I'll take care of your food education, but it would help if you decided to like chocolate. I want to collect two thousand pieces of aluminum wrapping paper by the year 2000."

Ernest would have liked to say what was going through his mind: "What a great ambition in aid of humanity!" After all, being in love doesn't mean you have to approve of everything.

Jeremy showered Ernest with smiles. So did Victoria's mother.

"This is my mother." She wanted to add "Your future mother-in-law," but this time, she managed to stop herself.

Ernest—where had he learned how to behave?—answered politely, "Good afternoon, Madame de Montardent, thanks for inviting me for lunch."

"Do call me Catherine. And please excuse the way I look. I've been unpacking boxes for weeks. I'm exhausted. But don't let that bother you, I spend my life that way."

Ernest looked carefully at this woman who had spent ten and a half years of her life pregnant, had had fourteen babies (maybe a world record), and despite it all seemed perfectly normal. What a difference from his own mother, who hadn't even managed to survive having one.

Catherine was neither old nor young. Victoria said she was forty-five. According to her daughter, she worked at some sort of government office, "like my dad." They had met as students. Ernest wondered where his own unknown parents had met, and how they had felt about each other. All these different people around him made more and more questions come to mind. Victoria looked like her mother, with her black hair held back by a red headband. They had the same fiery eyes, the same high cheekbones and expressive faces.

None of the brothers was home, except the baby. A

lady set a saucepan of boiling oil down in the middle of the vast table and Catherine said, "Thanks, Jeannette."

"What do you think of fondue?" Victoria asked, as everyone started boiling pieces of meat in the oil and then dipping them in the sauce. The enthusiasm called for a similar reply. Ernest was thinking of how disgusting Germaine would have found the bubbling sound of hot oil (oil—public enemy number one), the six different sauces to dip the meat in (sauce—public enemy number two), and the mountain of red meat (red meat—public enemy number three).

Ernest replied diplomatically, "It must be pretty tricky to eat like this with fourteen children. How do you manage when everyone's at home?"

"We're never all here at once," said Catherine, "but we can always put out more saucepans."

"Well, it's good. It's certainly interesting," said Ernest. "Thank you very much."

Victoria mashed a banana for Jeremy and handed it to Ernest. "I'm giving you the honor of feeding him . . . but only if you taste my chocolate truffles." Ernest tasted one, continuing the list in his head: "Sugar—public enemy number four."

*   *   *

Before they left, Catherine kissed her guest warmly. "Come eat here whenever you like."

"I think you have too many mouths to feed already."

"If there's enough for sixteen, there's enough for seventeen."

"Thanks. It's very kind of you, but Grandmother is all alone."

"Bring her with you. The more the merrier."

Ernest smiled. It was getting to be a habit. Victoria told her mother that she'd be home a little later than usual. Jeremy said, "Gaga."

After school, a big surprise—there were two apples on the table. Ernest told Victoria to sit down. She wolfed down the fruit. "It's amazing how good an apple can be. I'll have to try it with chocolate!"

"We'll sit here and do our homework."

"You'll have to explain everything. I couldn't figure out a thing." Ernest calmly went through the math problems, and the exercises in grammar and vocabulary. He was delighted to share what he had understood.

"I'm terribly behind," said Victoria in a low voice.

"You'll catch up. You learn quickly."

"I hope so. My brothers have never had time to explain anything to me. They just tell me I'm stupid. Hey! Let's forget this stuff for now. We've finished. Let's watch TV."

"There is no TV." He glanced at the wardrobe where the letter was hidden. He would have liked to show it to her, but just at that moment, Grandmother walked into the room.

Alphonse

On Sunday morning, Ernest's grandmother did not appear at the kitchen table. "That's twice now," thought Ernest. She wasn't exactly a fun companion, but Ernest couldn't imagine his life without her. It was somehow comforting to have her there every day. When he showed her his report cards, she would pat his head as if he were a little dog. All he could bring her from the outside world were his good grades. And now there was Victoria! Not to mention the chocolate croissants. Suddenly he was scared of finding her in her bedroom, lifeless.

He knocked on her bedroom door. What a relief to

hear her feeble "Yes?" He went in. She was lying there with the same pile of letters on her lap. She tried to hide them quickly under the pillow, but she couldn't do anything that quickly.

Ernest crept up to the bed, scared stiff, like a common soldier in front of a general. Somehow, his fear pushed him toward her.

"Grandmother, we've known each other for ten years, for my whole life, and I know absolutely nothing about you, about our family, my mother, my father. . . . I only know those strangers who stare at us out of the portraits on the walls. Take him for instance." Ernest pointed at a large photograph of a serious man who looked between thirty and forty. He was very handsome, though a little arrogant, as if he knew that his photo would be kept forever.

To his surprise, his grandmother answered quite simply, as if this single photo was the key to the doorway of conversation. "That's your grandfather, my husband, Alphonse. We only lived together for eight years. He died in battle in 1940. Your father was born after that. He never knew his father."

"Like me."

"Like you."

But instead of thinking about himself, he said, "You've had a really hard life, Grandmother."

"The deeper the pain, the harder it is to talk about."

"But what can you tell me about Alphonse?" He said "Alphonse" as a step on the way to saying "Gaspard," *his* father.

"I only have good things to say about him. We didn't have time to get tired of each other." She searched for her words. "He was tall, distinguished . . . a big man in every sense of the word . . . intelligent, witty, inspiring, and very, very handsome . . . like you. Like your father," she added inaudibly.

"Handsome is only what you see, it's not important. Tell me really, what was he like?"

"He was always in search of the truth. He wanted to get to the bottom of everything. He never lied to himself. He spent his time thinking."

"And what about these letters, Grandmother, the ones you read in bed?"

"I know them by heart, Ernest. They are the love letters Alphonse wrote me. He was too shy to tell me directly, so he wrote."

"But he's been dead for over fifty years. Do you still remember him?"

"Yes I do. Every day, every minute . . . but I can't touch him. And he can't touch me."

"And my father?" asked Ernest. They could talk about the dead, but what if the living were out of bounds? His grandmother pretended not to hear. He changed the subject. "Would you like me to bring your breakfast?"

"No, that won't be necessary. I'm getting up now. You can heat up some milk if you like."

Never before had they had such a long conversation. It had always seemed as if Grandmother had lived according to the proverb, "The mouth is a door which should remain closed." With his questions, Ernest had found a key to that door, and he had seen that opening it, even a crack, had done them both good. Grandmother seemed younger, less frail.

From the kitchen window Ernest saw a patch of blue sky and was suddenly seized by a crazy idea.

"Grandmother," he began, "are we poor?"

"Why do you ask that?"

"We hardly spend a cent."

"We have enough to live on, Ernest, but how much does anyone really need to live?"

"Grandmother, it's a lovely day. Let's get dressed and

go out. We'll walk around that beautiful square, and then go to the restaurant on the corner."

Taken aback, his grandmother sighed. "Oh, I couldn't do that. I'm old, Ernest, I'm tired. And you have to do your homework."

"Grandmother, I did my homework yesterday." His hopes were fading somewhat, but still he insisted. "Come on, Grandmother. It isn't right to stay shut up in this gloomy apartment." He repeated something Victoria had said: "Energy is like eating. Once you try a little, you get an appetite."

"Germaine has left us our lunch. We mustn't waste it. Besides, I haven't got the strength."

"Grandmother, you have to live . . . before you let yourself die."

Precious said no more. She finished her breakfast in silence, and walked out of the kitchen.

Ernest was disappointed. He got dressed and sat on the shabby sofa as usual with a book. But this habit had a slightly bitter taste. He found it difficult to follow the words in his book because his mind was buried under a cloud of misery.

When his grandmother reappeared wearing a black coat and a black hat and carrying a handbag worthy of a witch, she said, "You never ask me for anything. I suppose I can do this for you . . . just this once."

Ernest shut his book in jubilation, put on his coat, and took his grandmother's arm. They made a strange couple—they might have come from the pages of the book he had just closed, a book from another century.

The next day was Monday. The gray day seemed to have forgotten Sunday's sun. The teacher acted as if he were hung over—grumpy and irritable, even with Ernest. Instead of starting the week with his usual grammar lesson, he decided to use one of those old tricks which teachers reserve for days when they are feeling their laziest and most disagreeable. He gave out paper, and without even bothering to speak, wrote the word "Sunday" on the blackboard. He then mimed that this was the subject of the essay they were to write. Okay, so being a teacher isn't always the greatest job.

Ernest was in heaven, because for once, he really had something to say and didn't have to exhaust himself inventing a life. He flashed a grin at Victoria, got himself ready, held his pen at the top of the page, and made it cover the page with writing from top to bottom, as quickly as a grand prix racecar driver. And he was the winner, because when he parked his pen after the final stop, he saw that the others were still busy writing. The teacher was at his desk with his head in his hands, as if this were the only way he could keep it from rolling onto the floor. Victoria was writing frantically. She really did have all the luck—she could fill a whole page with nothing but her brothers' names. When the teacher collected the copies, he seemed to feel a bit better. As usual, he put Ernest's at the top of the pile so that by reading it first, he would have the strength to face the others. He read it aloud to the class.

Couscous Sunday

I have never been to a restaurant in my life. I have never been out on a Sunday. I have never eaten couscous. My grandmother has never been outside her apartment for as long as I have known her.

It is a great day when a "never" is erased. But when three "nevers" are erased in one day and are replaced by three "first times," that day is three times as great.

Yesterday, I went out with Grandmother to the restaurant on the corner to eat couscous.

Couscous is a North African specialty which is made from grains of wheat. The restaurant owner brought the couscous to our table in four parts. They were:

1) the couscous

2) the vegetable broth

3) the meat

4) the hot sauce

This is what you do: You put the couscous grains in a soup plate and make a little hill. On this you put the vegetables to make the scenery—carrots, turnips, and leeks, and chick peas, which look like little rocks. Then you add some meat and pour some broth over the whole plate. If you like things hot, you can add a little harissa, which is made from hot red peppers—they burn like the sun from their native land.

At first, Grandmother was scared to try, but she soon got into it. Each mouthful is a surprise. And it's so good to taste faraway flavors, and to be warmed up by a hot dish in the middle of winter. When you feel good, you get strength and energy. This was easy to see in my usually silent grandmother. She began to talk. She spoke of war and the dead, of loss and of pain. But talking about the dead brings them to life, and that must be better than letting them die a little more each day, buried in silence. Every time a word is spoken in their memory, they come to life, even if it is only a tear's worth.

And even for us, who really are alive, but who don't live fully, it may sound strange, but couscous, yes, couscous made me realize that it's never too late to learn how to live. But you need a good teacher and a lot of willpower. I really want to have willpower, so I can learn, not just skills like reading and writing that help to pass the time, but to really live, because afterward, you die, and then it's too late.

Grandmother had a hard time paying our bill. She thought it was expensive, and said that money is like a second skin for her, like part of her being. She read over the bill at least five times with her half-moon glasses and then she asked me to check it!

On the way home, we walked through the square. It was as if Grandmother had been there before, but in another life. Of course she knows it, because she has always lived close by. But she went straight to one of the benches, as if she owned it. We sat in silence as usual. But we were accompanied by the shared memory of a delicious meal, and the words we had spoken held a promise of future occasions when we might taste the spice of life in our humdrum existence.

When we got home, we passed a Chinese restaurant on the other side of our street. I said to Grandmother, "Let's try that one next." And Grandmother replied, "We'll see . . . let's just take one day at a time."

The class was silent and Ernest was ashamed to have given himself away. Victoria took his hand from his lap and raised it to touch her cheek.

It was then that Ernest remembered something else about the day before. For the first time, the letter had remained in its hiding place.

Dan

After class on that wintery Monday, Dan and Simeon were outside school waiting for Victoria in the family minivan.

"We get to do the shopping today. Ernest, you have to give us a hand. We're going to the huge supermarket in Bercy."

"I'd be glad to, but I have to let Grandmother know."

"We'll stop off at your place on the way so you can go and tell her."

Ernest had never been in a car, and driving around was a new source of enjoyment for him. Neither had he been inside even the local grocery store, and this supermarket seemed to him like another planet. Dan gave him a ten franc piece to rent a shopping cart. While he watched carefully how Victoria, Dan, and Simeon each put a coin in the slot, Victoria explained, "We need four shopping carts because we're like four families, get it?"

"Here's your list," said Dan, handing him a piece of paper covered with names of things to buy. "See you at the cash register in forty-five minutes."

Ernest's head was already spinning. He would have liked to spend all day scrutinizing all those boxes, packets, and bags he saw on the shelves, and the price tags, too. He had been to a museum on a school field trip, but this museum was much more exciting. There was so much to see . . . but he had to be quick.

Three packs of six quarts of milk . . . that made eighteen quarts . . . two packs of diapers, six dozen eggs . . . He went about it as he always did, methodically and conscientiously. His efficiency, even in this foreign country of the supermarket, got him to the bottom of the list before time was up. He made his way toward the book racks as if they were familiar territory. Leaning against the cart, he read the titles on the colorful covers.

His eyes ran from one book to another, and it was only when another shopping cart crashed into his own that he came back to earth. Luckily it was Dan's, over-flowing with all sorts of stuff. Dan picked up the fallen packets of cereal, cans of sweet corn, and underwear, muttering absently, "See you at the cash register."

Ernest pushed his shopping cart toward the central stand where the best-sellers were piled up. There something caught his eye. It was not the title of the book, but the name of the author. His eyes looked right through the cover. Paralyzed he gazed at it until he finally decided to grab hold of the book. It was certainly an unexpected place for this to happen, on a day remarkable for its ordinariness, when he had expected nothing in particular.

He turned it over and over, read a quarter of the blurb on the back without taking any of it in. He flipped through the pages from beginning to end, then from the end to the beginning. He rubbed the book against his forehead and hugged it to his chest without realizing that it was only an object made of paper, one that he had no money to buy, either. In any case, he didn't have to buy it. This book belonged to him.

He let himself slip down onto the floor to look at his book in comfort, and it was in this position that Victoria found him. In a complete panic and out of breath she

said, "We've been waiting for you for ten whole minutes. Are you trying to make us miss supper or what?"
Ernest barely raised his head. He hardly knew where he
was or what she was talking about. His cart had drifted
off, pushed right and left by other hurried shoppers.
Victoria held out her hands. "Up we go!" she said, as if
he were a baby she was trying to get up. Ernest shook
himself abruptly out of his stupor, and held the book up
to Victoria's eyes. Victoria, who liked the titles best, read
out loud, *"World War Two: Lessons from Our Fathers."*
She didn't notice the author's name.

"Oh you and your wars, Ernest. There's more to life
than wars you know! Come on, my brothers are running out of patience!"

Ernest kept hold of the book, grabbed the cart,
which was in the stationery section by now, and rushed
with Victoria toward the checkout line as if on skates.

Simeon was taking the contents out of his cart and
putting it onto the checkout counter, and then Dan was
putting things back into the cart after they were rung
up. Victoria added Ernest's cartful to the pile. The
people in line behind them started to look impatient,
especially when Ernest pushed in front of them. "This is
the first time he's ever been shopping," said Victoria by

way of explanation. She added, "He's a genius in school, but in the supermarket he's pathetic!"

Dan paid the astronomical bill for the four cartfuls. "What is this? Are you a restaurant?" asked the check-out girl.

"Not at all." Dan said. "If you must know, I'm the eldest of thirteen brothers and one sister, and as strange as it may sound, we all eat at least three times a day."

"You're not serious!" said the girl.

"Oh yes I am. When my parents saw how perfect and handsome and intelligent I was, they said, 'We have to make thirteen others like him.' Unfortunately, the others didn't turn out as good as the original." And he pointed at Victoria and Simeon. The girl, a pretty redhead with sexy makeup, was enchanted by the family spokesman.

Dan, far from being good-looking, was short and fat and prematurely balding. This made him look older than twenty-two. In spite of this, he was a great success with women, who liked his sense of humor, his warmth, and his charm. As for him, he only had eyes for Milène, a fellow student of history at the university.

When the last bag had been packed into the cart, Ernest followed the others out. A yell came from the check-out girl. "Hey, what about the book? Thinking of stealing it or what?"

Ernest looked at Victoria, who knew that he didn't have a penny to his name. Dan took the book and read out the author's name.

"Gaspard Morlaisse . . . some relation of yours?"

"Um . . . it's my father . . . I think."

"Well this guy's pretty famous. He's on my reading list at school. It looks interesting. I'll buy it, and I can lend it to you."

Do you really have to buy a book written by your own father? Was it his father? How many Gaspard Morlaisses could there be? Was it possible that Ernest, who until that moment had never really had a father, could suddenly have come up with one who was famous? Ernest was so busy wondering about all this, that he said nothing the whole time they were unpacking from the shopping carts to the minivan and later from the minivan to the apartment.

"Are you staying for supper?" asked Dan, whose turn to cook was Monday.

"No thanks. I'm leaving. Grandmother . . ." but he couldn't get himself to leave until he had asked his question.

"Um . . . Dan, tell me, how do you go about finding an author's address?"

"You write to the publisher. See, the name on the bottom of the cover. Here, you want to read it first?"

"Yes, thanks, if you don't mind," said Ernest, trying to hide his impatience by putting the book away in his schoolbag, far out of sight of his grandmother.

Simeon

Ernest took the book to bed with him, but he was too restless to read. It took him a long time to get to sleep . . . and then a long time to wake up. In fact it was Germaine who woke him, when she came to tell him what time it was. Quickly Ernest stashed the book in his schoolbag, and rushed tardily into another day.

By now it was quite late. And when Ernest got to the bottom of the stairs, he saw right away that Victoria was not alone. She was carrying a noisy wriggling bundle, and she looked disheveled and messy in a huge coat which must have been her mother's. Besides this, she was in a state of contagious panic.

She passed him the bundle saying, "Catch!" so Ernest

had no choice but to hold out his arms. He was re-warded with a resounding "Uh!" that came from the bundle, which was expressing gratitude in the only way it knew. At seven months, Jeremy had a monosyllabic but versatile vocabulary that covered every possible occurrence. Accompanied by a wide grin, "Uh!" meant that Jeremy was delighted by this unusual situation.

The de Montardents plus Jeannette constituted a large enough workforce to ensure that there was always someone on hand to look after the baby when the parents were at work. However, Tuesday was Jeannette's day off, and Simeon was on duty because he didn't have class. But Simeon had gone out on Monday evening, and hadn't come home. That morning, after each member of the family had gone on his carefree way, Victoria, the last to leave, found herself the sole owner of this eighteen-pound bundle of trouble.

She railed to Ernest, "That irresponsible good-for-nothing pig Simeon didn't even show up this morning!"

Ernest was more worried than Victoria that Simeon had disappeared. He said, "Maybe something happened to him . . ."

"To who?"

59

"To Simeon! Shouldn't we tell the police, or at least your parents?"

"You must be joking! It happens all the time with that numbskull. He's always going off. He thinks our place is overcrowded."

Ernest who, after all, didn't have much experience with such things, looked at Victoria in amazement. "And what are we going to do with *him?*" Jeremy meanwhile would not let go of Ernest's nose. He must have thought it was some kind of pacifier.

"Okay my little genius," she chanted to Jeremy. "What do you think? Wanna go to school?"

Jeremy replied with an enthusiastic, "Uh!"

"I don't think it's allowed. I think that if I were you, I'd stay at home."

"Oh sure, Ernest! You've never missed a day of school in your whole life! We have a test today, and I've studied so hard that I actually want to take it."

Ernest considered the situation while Victoria outlined her plan. "We'll hide him under my coat. If the teacher asks me why I don't take it off, I'll tell him I'm cold." Ernest went on thinking, while Jeremy tugged at his hair.

"Go on, move it! We can't be late, too! We mustn't draw attention to ourselves."

"He'll be hot, poor little guy."

"We'll all be hot!"

A few yards from the school, Victoria swapped Jeremy for the bottle and the diapers, which she gave to Ernest. He shoved it all into his schoolbag next to the heavy book which was loaded with the weight of his heart.

They tried to blend with the crowd in the playground, but Victoria looked like a camel from back to front. Ernest did his best to hide her, and whispered to Jeremy, "Don't be afraid, we're here. It's dark, it's hot, but it'll be over soon, my friend." Jeremy promised to be good with a solemn "Uh!"

No sooner had he taken up his position squashed between Victoria's knees and the desk, than Jeremy went back on his word. As soon as the teacher had given out the test papers, he started a quiet whimpering, which didn't go unnoticed by the students nearby.

"Pass me the bottle," whispered Victoria to Ernest.

Ernest leaned down to get it, but Victoria changed her plan. "Forget it. I think he's fallen asleep."

"Victoria, Ernest, quiet please." It was the first time that Ernest had ever been reprimanded, and he felt quite proud of the accomplishment. As he sat answering the questions on his test, Ernest wondered if he wasn't on the verge of beginning a career as a trouble-maker.

"Victoria, where do you think you are, Siberia?" asked the teacher. "Aren't you hot with that coat?"

Victoria shook her head without raising her eyes, and hoped that the teacher would forget about her. She was so hot that beads of perspiration were dropping onto her paper, but she was determined to show what she had learned with Ernest's help.

"Are you sure he's not suffocating?" Ernest whispered.

"Don't worry, he's used to it. He lived for nine months inside my mother's tummy."

As if to confirm Ernest's fears, Jeremy let out little snorting noises, which were followed by a terrible smell that spread through the classroom.

"Boy, that sure stinks," said Victoria.

"Ugh, I know. What do we do now?"

"Just keep working. He went number two, the little pig."

The test was almost over when Jeremy began

screaming. The coat was no use anymore, and Victoria had no choice but to let him out. The teacher would have had to be deaf, blind, and a complete imbecile not to have noticed. He walked toward the pair of kidnappers and calmly asked, "What's that?"

"It's my brother Jeremy, sir. Could you just hold him for one minute while I finish the test?"

The teacher accepted without hesitation. He walked Jeremy up and down by the window, rocking him gently. "Don't cry, little fellow," said the teacher. Jeremy obeyed instantly. It almost looked as if Jeremy might be good at this school business.

The principal didn't usually come into their class. She and the teacher didn't get along that well. However, today, she must have sensed something going on. Anyway, she caught the teacher, red-handed, with a baby in his arms—and this baby was not even in his class. "This is a school, not a nursery! What is this infant doing here? You are not permitted to babysit your own children in the classroom."

Jeremy beamed his agreement with an "Uh!"

Victoria went on writing, undisturbed. It was Ernest who leaped to his feet to explain. "There was no one to look after the baby this morning."

"This is not a daycare center. It is a public elementary school. Who is the owner of this baby?"

Ernest pulled Jeremy toward him. Victoria put her last period on the test paper and joined Ernest. "He's ours."

The principal stared poisoned daggers at them. This was the last straw.

"I mean, he's my little brother."

"Come with me!" ordered the principal. To the teacher she added, "I'll see you during recess."

"Excuse me, Madame," said Victoria, "but could we change him? He really needs it."

"Come with me this instant! I've already told you, this is not a daycare center!"

Ernest took his schoolbag to avoid having to pull out the diapers in front of everyone. The whole class was making frenzied gestures, and saying "ga-ga," "goo-goo," and other cute sounds babies like. Nobody can resist a baby . . . except the principal! The teacher had completely melted at the sight of Jeremy. He hadn't even thought of telling them they were in trouble.

The principal was another story. She didn't stop lecturing them. "In thirty years at school, this is the first time I have ever seen such a thing. Just wait till your parents hear about this."

Ernest realized that this was the first time he had seen the principal's office in his five years as a student.

"I am going to phone your families." Ernest didn't want to contradict her. She would have to learn the hard way that if she wanted to contact his "family" she would have to send a telegram.

"I will begin with you, Mademoiselle de Montardent," she announced disdainfully. She pulled out two files and dialed Victoria's number. No answer. She dialed Madame de Montardent's office number, saying loudly, "Office of Foreign Affairs." They heard a dozen rings through the loudspeaker, then a recorded message, then the crackle of recorded music.

Jeremy had stopped being so quiet. He wriggled, and protested. He made it clear with a grumpy "Uh!" that he didn't like the principal.

"Please, can we change him now?"

"I suppose so," came the disgusted answer, just as the bell rang for recess.

Victoria led the way to the girls' room, with Jeremy in her arms and Ernest in tow carrying a diaper.

"I can't come in there with you," protested Ernest, embarrassed by the girls crowding around them.

"Okay, let's go to the boys' room then. After all, Jeremy is a boy, and anyway, it's not as if I've never seen a weenie."

Victoria did her clean-up job, and they returned to the office, where they found the principal at the end of her tether.

"Your mother is in a meeting, your father is in a meeting, and I can't find the Morlaisses' phone number. Just what am I supposed to do?"

"He's a good boy, Madame. He won't be any trouble."

"He *is* trouble! *You* are trouble! That's it. You can just go home and look after the little brat there. I want to see your parents on Wednesday morning before school starts, otherwise you will not set foot in here again."

Feeling defeated, Ernest got his things and took Jeremy from Victoria. They walked together to her house, worried about what had just happened.

What a coincidence! They arrived at the same time as—Simeon, who greeted them with a cheery, "Hi there!" as if nothing had happened.

"Hi there yourself!" retorted Victoria bluntly.

"No school today?" he asked innocently. He took Jeremy from Ernest's arms, saying, "So my little be-bop baby's been out for a stroll?"

Victoria shrugged and asked Ernest, "What do you do with people like this? This guy jeopardized our entire future, and then he shows up like everything's fine. I bet he doesn't even know what day of the week it is."

"Oh no! Is it Tuesday? Already? Oh hell! Oh dear! What did you do with him?"

"He came to school."

"And Mom and Dad? Do they know?"

"They will soon enough!"

Jeremy was not at all pleased to be back home. He preferred school. "I'm going to get you something to eat," said Simeon, taking the situation in hand, not even realizing the problems his forgetfulness had caused.

"Hang on, I've got the bottle." Ernest opened his schoolbag to reveal total disaster. The bottle had leaked all over the book—the one thing he treasured more than anything in the world. He picked up the empty bottle and the book with sticky milk all over the pages.

Victoria immediately understood how serious this was, and she acted fast. "Don't worry, Ernest, we'll wash it and dry it with the hair dryer." While Simeon took care of the baby, Ernest and Victoria were in the bathroom giving the book emergency first-aid treatment.

Simeon felt his conscience pricking him. "I'll take you two back to school, and I'll explain everything."

"She said she wanted our *parents*. She'll tear you to pieces."

"Well, if you can't go to school, then I'll treat you to a movie."

Victoria kissed her daydreamer of a big brother. "Yeah!" she said. "What do you think we should see?"

Monsieur de Montardent

Ernest could have added seeing a movie to his list of "firsts." This time he didn't have to be asked to write an essay. He wanted to commit this adventure to paper. After all he wouldn't be able to tell his grandmother about it without also telling her about how he had been thrown out of school. He believed what Monsieur de Montardent had said when he had arrived home. "Don't worry. It's not worth troubling your grandmother. I'll fix everything on Wednesday morning."

So with peace of mind, Ernest wrote about the movie:

Victoria paid for two tickets at the entrance. We walked into a dark room where the only light came from a huge screen. I was a little nervous, especially since the volume was turned up loud, and the scenes looked violent.

"It's just the previews," said Victoria. We were practically the only people there in the middle of the afternoon, and we sank into the comfortable seats. I was thinking about what had happened that morning. I checked to make sure that my book was nice and dry in my bag, and I was so comfortable that I was almost ready to fall asleep when the movie began. Then, suddenly, everything else left my head. I was completely captivated by what I saw before my eyes. I escaped from my own life, and it felt great. When it was all over, I stumbled a little coming out of the theater as I realized that the school day was over, and that this ordinary Tuesday would continue on its way as I would on mine. But I secretly hoped it would never catch up with me.

Ernest left Victoria in front of her building after the movie. That's where he had met Monsieur de Montardent for the first time. Victoria's father explained that Simeon had told him everything, and said that on Wednesday he would go with them to school.

Ernest felt sort of strange. He was still under the movie's spell, which he liked, but he also felt weighed down by a feeling that something was missing. He went home, ate his apple, and realized what it was: his everyday companion, his homework! He had nothing to do, and he had left all his books in the classroom. He closed his bedroom door, took out the injured book, turned the pages, and read: "For Jennifer, Myrtle, Clementine, Cherry, and Peach." At least one name was definitely missing from this dedication. He felt a shock, and instead of reading the book, he wrote a letter for the first time in his life.

> *Dear Monsieur Morlaisse,*
>
> *I was very interested in your book. I mean, I didn't exactly buy it for the writing. You see, what I found the most interesting was your name, because . . . it's the same as mine.*
>
> *I don't want you to feel sorry for me. David Copperfield and Oliver Twist had a much worse time than me. In fact, I didn't even realize how uninteresting my life was*

until I met Victoria, a girl in my class. That's
when I discovered that life could be more
rich and exciting than I ever imagined. Since
then, I have tasted a delicious fondue, I have
held an adorable baby in my arms, I have
discovered the supermarket experience (actu-
ally, that's where I found your book), and I
have managed, by sheer force of my own
willpower, to get my grandmother to leave
the house and come as far as the restaurant
on the corner to eat couscous. I don't know
if, when I was a baby, anyone kissed and
hugged me as much as they do my little
friend Jeremy, but I would say I got my very
first kisses from Victoria, who is always kiss-
ing me hello and good-bye and swearing
that we will get married in exactly thirteen
years, eight months, and three days.

I'm ten years old. I'm in fifth grade, and
until today, I was a really good student.
Grandmother doesn't say too much, but I
think she has always been pleased with me. I
hope she never finds out that I was thrown
out of school today.

For a very long time, I barely realized that
other kids all have mothers and fathers,

brothers and sisters. I didn't have much to do with other kids. I've been trying to find out more about my family, but Grandmother is very quiet. One thing she did tell me was that my father was still alive. Could this father be you? I really don't know what to hope for, but please, Monsieur Morlaisse, I hope to hear from you.

Yours sincerely,
Ernest Morlaisse

Ernest looked in every drawer of every bureau before finally coming across a yellowed envelope whose flap didn't stick. He wrote the name *Gaspard Morlaisse* on the front, stuck down the flap with Scotch tape, and hid the letter in the book in his schoolbag awaiting the fateful next day.

Victoria and her father were waiting for him, double parked in front of his building. They honked as soon as he appeared. Monsieur de Montardent looked the part in his business suit, but seemed slightly rattled by an extra task on his crowded agenda. He looked tired. In fact he looked exhausted, like someone who had never asked God or Santa Claus or even the stork to bless him with fourteen children.

Ernest didn't know how babies were made. Neither Grandmother nor Germaine had ever told him. He didn't want to ask Victoria, because he was afraid she might actually know, and she would fill him in on all the gory details. However it was done, it couldn't be that hard, because people of the most basic intelligence had managed to do it since the dawn of time. Maybe there were certain things that a person didn't have to learn how to do, maybe certain things came automatically, for example, eating, sleeping . . . and loving Victoria.

As usual, the principal was in a bad mood—very upset and nervous. But when she set eyes on Monsieur de Montardent, she was completely transformed to sugar and spice. He was impeccably dressed, like a chic Italian, with a haircut to match. He was tall and slim, and though not exactly handsome, he had a distinguished face. Above all, he had the natural authority of a leader. Even before she had said a word, the principal felt guilty for wasting the time of such a man. On the phone, she had been impossible, hammering him with, "I will not tolerate such behavior!" However, finding herself face to face with him, all she could say was, "It is really of no importance, sir, these things can happen to anybody." She even assured him that she would personally see to it that Victoria and Ernest made up the afternoon they had missed, and that their grades would not suffer as a result. She was so overpowering with her "excuse me's" and her "sorry's" that Victoria's father couldn't even get a word in. He was almost disappointed, like someone who prepares for a bomb and gets hit by cotton balls. He kissed the children goodbye, and hurried away to his office.

Victoria and Ernest were given a hero's welcome by their classmates and the teacher. He gave them back their tests. Perfection! Jeremy had been a good-luck charm!

One of the three girls in class named Elodie invited them to her birthday party, and Ludovic asked Ernest to play football at break. Ernest had become less of an outcast, but he still didn't know how to play football.

One can get used to anything, Ernest had learned, and already he was getting used to being sociable. But the more he spoke with people outside his home, the more he longed to speak to his grandmother inside. Without alarming her, he wanted to tell her about Jeremy at school, and to show her the book. Ernest felt determined to talk to her, and at lunchtime he walked into the apartment to do it. But when he got there, he found it more silent than the empty movie theater. In the kitchen, he saw that the table had not been set, and that no pot was heating on the stove. Even these tiny lights from his old life had gone out. Only the bag of vegetables for the soup was on the counter. He rushed into Grandmother's room. The bed was unmade, and its occupant had disappeared.

He thought of his letter, wondering if maybe it had brought down a thunderbolt, but he knew that he hadn't even mailed it. He walked around in circles. He looked for the other hidden letters, as if some scribbled fragments could solve the mystery. He had no idea what to do, besides going to get Victoria to help him. But what if he left and his grandmother came back while he was out? She would be sick with worry!

Worry himself sick. That's what Ernest proceeded to do. He sat on the lumpy sofa and surrendered to a terror that poisoned his brain and prevented him from being able to move. He sat there motionless, without reading, without thinking, just listening to the echo drumming endlessly through his head: "Grandmother is dead."

The fifth time around, when the dreadful phrase had sunken in so completely that he believed it, his grandmother, fully dressed, walked into the living room, sat down next to him, and said, "Germaine had a heart attack. We went to the hospital in an ambulance. The neighbor called for it. She's going to have heart surgery, right away." Then Ernest saw something he had never seen. His grandmother burst into tears.

Ernest gathered the fragile bony creature in his arms, and instead of saying, "Don't cry," he said, "Cry, Grandmother, cry."

She whispered, "Deep down I always knew that one day there would be no one to take care of you. When you get to eighty, you know you can't go on forever, but I just couldn't admit it."

Then she pulled herself together and said, "Come on, let's have something to eat, and I'll take you to school. Then I'll do a bit of shopping for dinner."

"I can do the shopping after school, Grandmother."

"I don't know how we'll manage, Ernest. I'm too old, and you're too young."

"Don't worry, Grandmother. We'll manage somehow."

"And Germaine . . ."

"Did it really hurt?"

"Yes, but now she's sleeping, and they told me that—"

Ernest finished the sentence, "She won't be able to work anymore."

"And Ernest, I haven't got the strength."

"We'll share mine, Grandmother."

Henrietta

"You can come and live at my house!" suggested
Victoria. "I've got a mattress under my bed."

"And what about Grandmother?"

"I'll ask my mother. I'll let you know tomorrow. I've
told you, Ernest, if there's room for seventeen, there's
room for eighteen."

"Well I think Grandmother needs peace and quiet.
She isn't used to so many people."

"We could give her the maid's room."

"I don't really think that's a great idea. We'll be okay.
If you could just lend me a recipe book, I'll start learn-
ing how to cook."

Ernest dug into his schoolbag and pulled out the letter he had written. He held it out to her. "Say, Victoria, Dan told me he'd find the publisher's address."

"Sure, sure. Don't worry, Dan'll get it."

After picking up a few groceries near school, Ernest found his grandmother in the kitchen, peeling vegetables. She took so long over each carrot and each potato, you'd have thought she was creating sculpture. When he sat beside her he saw that peeling vegetables was not as easy as he had thought. Even breaking eggs turned out to be much harder than it looked. He hoped Grandmother would like the omelette with pieces of eggshell in it. He so wanted to make the meal a success and prove to Grandmother that they would be able to manage.

Making soup was feasible. You just threw vegetables into a pot of water and let them swim. But Grandmother hovered in front of the stove anxiously, as if she wanted to make sure they didn't drown. Ernest sat at the table to do his homework. He knew that Grandmother would be reassured to see that life went on as usual, and Ernest liked being in the same room with her.

He put his books away in his schoolbag—right next

to his book, which lay there like a rumbling volcano. He had only put out one of the two soup bowls when the front doorbell rang. Victoria and Zebulun rushed into the kitchen with a cooking pot and a cake.

"It's beef stew," said Zebulun, who was only a year older than Victoria, but considered himself far superior, since he was in sixth grade.

"But you shouldn't have," said Grandmother, truly embarrassed by such generosity. "We're doing just fine. . . ."

"We make everything on an industrial scale, so don't worry, Madame Morlaisse . . . it doesn't cost us any more . . . and we'll keep you company. We'll eat with you."

Ernest looked for extra plates, but his grandmother went straight into the living room to get her best china, which Ernest had never seen. She was even smiling.

Sitting down in front of the steaming stew with the pretty china on the table and Grandmother smiling made the crisis they were going through seem a hundred miles away.

"So, we've been talking," said Victoria excitedly. "Jeannette has a daughter who is looking for a job, and she'd be happy to come and replace Germaine for you. I've never seen her, but Jeannette says she's pretty wild."

"Is that a good thing?" whispered Ernest.

"How old is she?" asked Madame Morlaisse.

"She must be about twenty."

"It wouldn't hurt to have someone young around here for once."

"Apparently, she loves to cook. She wanted to be a chef, but she couldn't stand cooking school. They didn't let her make the things she wanted. Her dream is to open a restaurant."

"There's not much cooking here with just the two of us."

"But she's happy to do anything, and she knows how to sew, too."

"Well then, if she would like to come and meet us tomorrow . . . we'll see."

She turned up just before Ernest left.

"I'm Henrietta," said the giant, who was even taller in her five-inch heels. Ghoulish makeup covered her eyelids in gray-black. Her hair looked like a black vulture's nest. This black head appeared from out of a skintight fluorescent orange dress which was so short that it was

82

more of a bathing suit perched on top of legs as long as stilts. Ernest couldn't help noticing the breasts, which lurched toward him like a pair of cannons. He had a feeling that the whole get-up would not be to his grandmother's liking, but he was wrong. His grandmother was blind to everything but the energy and the smile.

"Ay yi yi, it's so dark in here," said Henrietta. "Let's get a bit of light on the subject."

For once Ernest didn't want to hurry off to school. He would have liked to stay and watch Henrietta, who seemed like a little girl who had just been given the dollhouse of her dreams.

When Ernest arrived home for lunch, he was greeted by heavenly smells wafting through the door. Usually he wasn't hungry, but today he followed his nose to the kitchen, where he wanted to plunge his entire head into the bubbling sauce.

"To begin with, we've got a little salad with pine nuts, then we're having coq au vin. The dessert's a surprise!" His grandmother arrived at the table dressed up in a ballgown from another era. When she saw Ernest's reaction, Henrietta declared, "This isn't a hospital! No one eats *my* cooking wearing a bathrobe."

Although Precious had complied with the dress

code, she found it difficult to eat these weird dishes. She tasted everything with the caution of a king who thought he was about to be poisoned. She was suspicious of each spoonful of foreign substance, but little by little, taste by taste, her resistance gave way to an avalanche of pleasure.

Delicious was too feeble a word to describe that lunch. Ernest realized that he would be in need of additional adjectives. Before leaving, Henrietta whispered, "Your grandmother has asked me to make soup for tonight. It's broccoli and spinach. You heat it up, and stir in the croutons and garlic. Tomorrow I'll make veal stew."

With each day came more surprises. The next day, Ernest arrived home to find that all the curtains had been taken down, some of the furniture and ornaments had disappeared, and some of the things in his own room had been moved.

His grandmother answered his unasked question. "Henrietta says that this is a home, not a flea market." She seemed to enjoy telling him about her day. "This magic housekeeper doesn't stop talking; she's always asking me what I prefer—pepper or cumin, garlic or ginger—she's already spent four times as much as Germaine on food."

"But it's at least four times better."

"She swears that this is just the beginning, to get in what she calls "the vital minimum stock." Tomorrow she wants to drag me to the shops to choose new curtain material but I absolutely refuse! Anyway, tomorrow I'm going to visit Germaine."

"Can I come with you?"

"Oh, in that case, we'll go after school."

When Henrietta arrived, she was wearing fluorescent yellow with the same high heels. She was out of breath from carrying the sewing machine, the shopping bags, and various other packages. Once again, Ernest regretted leaving the apartment.

When he got home, there were new curtains. They had tiny flowers and fruit printed on a pale yellow background. They changed everything. "A great choice, Grandmother. It looks so nice."

"It wasn't me. I told Henrietta to go ahead and choose for us. Eat your snack and we'll go."

The snack was a slab of chocolate cake left over from dessert the previous evening. But even that didn't manage to quell Ernest's apprehension at the idea of seeing Germaine in a hospital.

At the entrance to the room, a nurse told Ernest that he couldn't go in. Grandmother had to put on a mask, a cap, and a long paper gown. Ernest helped her on with this garb and watched her approach the bed with small steps.

Germaine's eyes were closed. There was one tube coming out of her nose, and another from under the blanket. She had no makeup on. She looked fragile. Grandmother touched her and spoke. "Germaine, we are so sorry that you aren't feeling well, but you'll see, it'll get better and better. You are strong, Germaine, you'll get over this. We're thinking of you. We're on your side. Don't worry about us either, Germaine, we're managing. Everything's fine, and if you like, when you come out we'll fix you up a nice room at home, you can rest and we'll all be together."

Ernest was amazed. He had never heard Grandmother talk to Germaine like this, so informally. Maybe people who were ill needed to be treated differently. Or maybe it was Henrietta's influence. She spoke like this to his grandmother, and Grandmother in turn had become less formal so as not to offend her.

Germaine opened her eyes and said, "Ernest?"

"He came with me, but children aren't allowed in. He's over there, behind the door."

Ernest felt a tugging at his heartstrings at exactly the same moment as his heart sent out an urgent message. Up until this moment he had not thought of it. He had seen Germaine practically every day of his life. It was only now that the idea occurred to him that she might die. She was not the best cook in the world, she didn't bring vast improvements to their everyday life, but she did belong to their life, and to their hearts. He thought of her from time to time at school. When he worked hard he would say to himself, "Germaine will be pleased." She wasn't the type to kiss and cuddle, but that smile of hers (expressly reserved for him) so often seemed to show that she was holding back, as if she felt that the world was no place for demonstrations of affection. He liked the way she said "Ernest." He liked her face, florid as it was with makeup. He liked the way she insisted on the importance of having principles. When all was said and done, in fact, he loved her. He gazed at her through the glass panel, and cried.

Benjamin

Ernest and Precious soon became accustomed to this burst of spice that Henrietta brought to their lives. For Ernest, life was suddenly full of surprises, and he learned that something new and marvelous could happen every single day. The first, and most marvelous thing, had been Victoria, and other minor, medium, and magnificent marvels had followed. Ernest woke up looking forward to each day, just wondering more and more what would happen next. It was as if he had been living at the wrong time, with a dead mother, a missing father, a panic-stricken grandmother, and an anxious Germaine, and he himself had been half asleep, like

Sleeping Beauty, waiting for Princess Charming to wake him up for his real life.

He would wait for Henrietta until the last possible instant, before leaving for school, waiting to hear her high heels clicking on the landing. But one day, she didn't arrive, and Ernest had to leave without saying hello. That day he returned to a house where no delicious new dish was bubbling on the stove. That evening, he had to eat leftovers with a mopey, silent grandmother.

Victoria had not been at school, and Ernest didn't feel like talking either. As for Henrietta, he merely thought, "Something must have come up." It was fifteen-year-old Benjamin de Montardent who came to tell them that Henrietta had the flu, as did Victoria, Zebulun, and Jeremy. Henrietta didn't want to give them her germs.

When Henrietta came back to the empty household, she was even thinner than before. That's when she began to rant and rave. "This place is completely insane. Don't you get it? Look at this paper, read the date! See, it says we are in the twentieth century—in fact nearly in the twenty-first! But in this crazy house you'd think it was 1850, or even the dark ages. I swear it, I cannot go on working here without a phone! It's completely impossible. First I had to get hold of the family my mother works for, and then they had to come all the way over here to tell you. I mean there are emergencies in life! God forbid you would like to call up and see how poor old Henrietta is doing on her deathbed. God forbid you get the urge to say something like, 'Henrietta, take care of yourself and get well soon.' "

Ernest had never witnessed a hysterical fit. He wasn't sure how his grandmother would react. He worried that she might reject this brilliant being who wanted to reorganize their world. But his grandmother just gave in. "All right. We'll see to it."

So it was that, with Henrietta's help, a light gray telephone found a home on the living-room dresser—the same dresser as the neglected letter. Henrietta made a list of three phone numbers in a notebook—her own, the de Montardents' and the emergency number. Ernest liked picking up the receiver just to hear the dial tone. He would pat the phone, as if encouraging it to speak. Somewhere out there, on the other end of the line, someone had to be there, a voice to talk to . . . a father.

Henrietta gave him a brief lesson in the art of the phone call and Ernest used Victoria's number to practice. The voice, hoarse from a hacking cough, was not hers.

"Is this Victoria de Montardent?"

"What's left of her. . . ."

"What's the matter?"

"I am a victim of poisonous bacteria which have traveled into my bronchial tubes and are about to enter my nervous system. I have a fever, I feel weak, and I am infectious!"

"Is it serious?"

"Not as long as I can still eat chocolate. It's the best medicine. At this point, half the family is sick. It's like a hospital here."

"What can I do for you?"

"Hey, wait a minute! I just realized that you're *calling* me! Are you in a phone booth?"

"I'm at home. We got a phone."

"I don't believe it!"

"It's because of Henrietta."

"Ernest, I'm nervous. You're getting too modern. You're going to end up the same as everyone else."

"Nobody is the same as everyone else!"

"Everybody is the same as everyone else!"

"We're both right."

"Give me your number. I still can't believe it. . . . I have to make sure it's true. I'll call you right back."

When Victoria called back, the shrill sound of the phone ringing made everyone jump. They were so petrified that it took fifteen rings before anyone thought of answering.

At the other end, Victoria, in professor mode, lectured him, "When the telephone rings, you have to answer it."

From the moment it arrived, the telephone took up far more space than its twenty-five square inches, for Ernest was always ready to pounce on it like a worried mother listening for her baby's cry. The telephone had a life of its own, and considerably increased the "surprise potential" of a day. In the evening, Ernest and Precious would sit in front of the telephone like some people sit in front of the fireplace or the television. Ernest prayed to this seemingly deaf God to give some electronic sign of its existence; but they didn't know many people, and Victoria was too worn out to call all the time.

In the morning, Ernest would walk by, saying goodbye to the phone sadly, and in the evening he would run to see it as soon as he opened the door. He looked up the name Morlaisse in the phone book which had come with the monster, and he immediately discovered that one Gaspard Morlaisse lived in a neighborhood that was tantalizingly and dangerously nearby. He learned the phone number by heart and with difficulty resisted the temptation to dial.

Each time he managed to stop himself from calling Gaspard, he rewarded himself by calling Victoria. And each time, Benjamin answered, greeting Ernest like a long-lost friend with a heartfelt, "How are you?" Ernest never knew what to say after, "Fine thanks, and you?" but Benjamin did. He was never at a loss for words, and he talked about everything under the sun. He told Ernest the latest about his family, the neighbors, the news, and sometimes he told Ernest about the stamps he had just bought for his collection. Ernest knew nothing about stamps, but nevertheless, he enjoyed sharing Benjamin's enthusiasm.

The de Montardent children had inherited their parents' physical characteristics: there were blue eyes from the father, brown eyes from the mother, dark brown hair, light brown hair, and other shades as well. But with Benjamin, the genes had really gone wild. He was the only one to have hair like red fire and eyes like green emeralds, along with a personality as calm as a white flag. He could spend hours at his desk quietly rearranging his stamps, but he was always the one who jumped up to answer the phone and shower his greetings on the world.

He was the black sheep of the boys, because he was the only one who was not a genius in school. He had learned to read from his stamps, he had learned geography from his stamps, and he liked history, nature, and literature because of what he saw on stamps. He also loved putting these minuscule pictures in the right spots in the stamp albums which people gave him every time there was an occasion for a present.

Benjamin begged for stamps from everyone he met, even from Ernest. "If you ever get an interesting letter, don't forget to show me."

"Sorry, but the postman has never once in my life had anything for me. Postal strikes don't strike me at all."

Ernest had begun looking in the mailbox since he had sent a letter himself. Two days after this conversation, in the little box he found a rectangular envelope addressed to Monsieur Ernest Morlaisse. It was stamped with a very ordinary stamp. Ernest's heart started beating hard against his chest, and pearls of sweat broke out on his forehead. He dared not open it. He went up to his room, took off the tie that still adorned his shirt, and sat down on the bed. He delicately unstuck the flap, and took a deep breath to prevent himself from exploding. He read:

> *Dear Ernest,*
> *Hello! Happy birthday! Happy New Year.*
> *Merry Christmas. Good luck. Have a good*
> *trip. Be well! Happy Easter. Have a good day!*
> *May all your wishes come true.*
> *I hereby declare, Ernest, my friend, that I*
> *remain your humble and most obedient ser-*
> *vant.*
> *Yours sincerely,*
> *All my love,*
> *your friend Benjamin*
>
> *P.S. You told me you'd never gotten a letter in*
> *your life. Well, you have now!*

Elodie

He arrived at school to find a second letter on his desk. When it rains it pours. "It is with pleasure that I invite you to my birthday party." On the invitation was a picture of a birthday cake and balloons, then the address, the time, and a note at the bottom: "Don't forget, you promised to come. Elodie."

Ernest remembered that Elodie had invited him with Victoria, but he didn't remember saying yes. He wasn't used to so much going on, though from now on he had decided to go with the flow. If someone invites you, go. If you can meet new people, go right ahead! For what could be more incredible, amazing, and fascinating than another human being? Ernest had made up his mind to make up for his first ten years. Anyway, Victoria would be there.

Victoria had been sick for a week, and Ernest felt that half of him was missing without her. He kept completely to his side of the desk they shared in class. Not so much as an elbow would cross the border in case he squashed her ghost. Ernest treated Victoria's absence like a hole in the ground which you walk around to avoid falling in. But you end up thinking so hard about the hole that you fall in anyway. There were a thousand things he wanted to tell her, and a thousand more things about her that he missed. School had become an empty place for Ernest.

They say that no one is indispensable.

"They're wrong," thought Ernest. "Everyone is indispensable and irreplaceable, at least for their parents!" He didn't know how his mind had led him to parents, especially since he didn't have any. Sometimes he would have liked to unplug his brain.

Since Victoria's absence, and even before, Elodie had been hanging around him. She kept on bringing him pieces of cake and little presents—a heart-shaped eraser, a smiley-faced marble, a pencil made from a twig. Ernest was horribly embarrassed. To refuse would be offending her, but he felt that she liked him more than he liked her. Sure, she was friendly, sociable, but she wanted to be his friend at any cost. She wanted him to love her! He simply couldn't return her feelings. Friendship can't be made to order. Either it's there or it isn't. If it does happen, then it's a sort of miracle.

He didn't like the way she persuaded the teacher to let her change her seat, saying that Christopher was always bothering her. He wasn't happy that she managed to get herself seated right beside him. For Ernest, seeing someone else in Victoria's place was betrayal. He found it repugnant and shrank into himself so that she wouldn't even brush against him.

She got hold of his phone number and called him every night to remind him about her party on Saturday. He didn't know how he could get out of it. On the other hand, even if he didn't like Elodie, she was a person after all, and she had feelings just like everyone else.

Victoria was still sick. She forbade him to visit. "Watch it! This place is alive with germs, but Mom says if I don't have a temperature over the weekend, I can go back to school on Monday. You'll have your work cut out for you helping your friend the turtle catch up."

"No point in rushing things. Haste makes waste."

"Ernest Shakespeare, you must be the most intellectual ten-year-old in the whole country."

"I'm certainly the most irritated, with this miserable birthday party."

"What did you get her?"

"What did I get her?"

"Sure, you have to get someone a present for her birthday." Ernest had never had birthday presents.

"I didn't think of that." The only idea he had was to get her a book.

"What about a book?"

"Elodie never reads."

"Maybe that's because she's never had a decent book."

"You could give her candy. She's always eating candy. I've got an even better idea. Tomorrow I'll make chocolate truffles. One of the boys will bring them over."

"No, don't bother. I'll think of something."

"It's no trouble. Plus it'll give me more aluminum foil for my collection."

Ernest went to the party feeling confident. "After all, this is a civilized country. How bad can it be?" His grandmother didn't really approve of his going out like this, but all she said was, "You're growing up." She repeated it like it was a curse. Her own father had grown up to go to war, her husband too. Neither had returned. Her son had grown up to disappear. Growing up meant splitting up, vanishing. Who knew if Ernest wouldn't be whisked away by the kids at the party?

He rang the bell and handed over Victoria's contribution, the truffles.

"Thank you," said Elodie without opening the packet.

There were none of the balloons, lights, or confetti promised on the invitation. There was just a huge living room, empty and bare in its luxury.

Only Elodie was decorated. She was made up, dressed up like a sixteen-year-old. She even had on high heels, not as high as Henrietta's, but definitely not flat. Ernest wondered if it was going to be a fancy party.

Ernest was unworldly, but he knew enough about life to realize that he was the first to arrive.

"Sit down," said his hostess. He thought that maybe Elodie had no parents either, but he dared not ask. It seemed like she lived in this gigantic apartment all by herself.

"What would you like to drink? Whisky, port, a martini?"

Thanks to his contact with Victoria, Ernest had begun to recognize a joke when he saw it.

"No thanks, I'm not thirsty."

"Go on, just a drop." She opened a cupboard filled with bottles and poured an amber colored liquid into two glasses. He realized now that she was not joking. She clinked her glass against Ernest's with a resounding, "Cheers!"

Out of politeness, he tasted it, and found that he couldn't swallow. Elodie, on the other hand, took little sips. Ernest had nothing to say and hoped desperately that the others would arrive soon.

She broke the ice. "So, what's new?"

There was so much new in his life that the words got caught in his throat like a traffic jam, and all he could say was, "It's a nice place you've got here."

"My mother redoes the living room every two months. At the moment she's into naked space. Would you like a pistachio?"

"No thanks," said Ernest, looking at the door. "I must be early."

"No, no. You're right on time."

"What about the others?"

"I don't like big parties. I prefer twosomes."

"But you invited Victoria and the rest of the class, didn't you?"

"When I found out that Victoria was sick, I cancelled with everyone else. It's the ideal opportunity for us to get to know each other."

"But we do know each other. We see each other every day."

"But not just the two of us."

To break the silence that followed Ernest said, "Victoria made the chocolate truffles I brought."

"Oh! Victoria. Don't you find that girl a bit bossy?"

"Bossy?"

"Yes, you know, she pushes herself."

"Lucky she does. If only I was a bit more pushy. . . . She's so natural. She's original. She's really *alive!*"

"She's a jerk."

Ernest felt as if he had just been punched in the stomach. Hurt, he stared at Elodie. His eyes begged for an explanation.

"You know, she only got friendly with you because she felt sorry for you. That's what she tells everyone. 'Poor Ernest, he's got no mother or father, no brothers or sisters, and he lives in a tomb.'"

"So you know everything?"

"If Victoria knows, everyone knows. If you don't believe me, ask the whole class."

"If you already know everything about me, I don't think we really need to get to know each other any better."

"But you still don't know anything about *me!*"

"I think I know all I want to know. Good-bye."

Issachar

Despite Victoria's warnings about contamination, Ernest rushed to her house after leaving Elodie. The door was opened by twenty-one-year-old Issachar, with a stethoscope around his neck and a mask over his mouth. This made it almost impossible to understand his greeting: "Anyone who comes in here is risking instant death." Issachar was a medical student, but he thought of himself already as the surgeon general. Sometimes having a little knowledge gives people big ideas. Issachar adored explaining the latest on all sorts of diseases: hepatitis, cancer, AIDS, multiple sclerosis, heart conditions, and dozens of bodily dysfunctions. However, his pet subject was psychiatry, and his conversations were always peppered with references to neuroses, psychoses, paranoiacs, manic depressives, and narcissists. His favorite expression was, "It's pathological, chronic, and congenital."

He would take his brothers' blood pressure, and diagnose the merest symptom as an incurable illness. As a little boy, his favorite game was doctor. He would put casts and slings on his faithful patients whether they had anything wrong or not. He made pills out of leftovers from the fridge rolled between his fingers. The members of the household were his involuntary subjects.

He took off his mask and thrust it over Ernest's face saying, "I'm already immune."

Ernest enjoyed being in this house where there were so many brothers that they even treated strangers like brothers. It was enough to walk into the house to be considered part of the fraternity.

"Victoria's asleep. She thinks that if she sleeps for two days, she'll be ready to go back to school on Monday. I'll go and see if she's up."

"No, don't wake her."

The de Montardents were making such a racket that the TV had to be turned up really loud to be heard.

Ernest had watched TV at school, but never as much as he would have liked, and he was certain that his grandmother had never set eyes on one. In the living room Dan, Benjamin, and Issachar were sitting on cushions in front of the TV. Benjamin, apparently fascinated by the program, held Jeremy on his knee. The baby was motionless although his nose, eyes, and mouth were running.

"Ernest, come and see!" called Dan. "It's interesting." Dan's eyes moved back and forth from the screen to Ernest and from Ernest to the screen, as Ernest tried to catch what he was saying.

"It's a show about history. They invite historians and living authors," added Benjamin.

"They can't very well invite dead ones," croaked Victoria, who had woken up and ambled into the living room in her pajamas. Between coughing fits, she caught sight of Ernest and looked astonished.

"What are you doing here? Didn't you go to Elodie's?"

"I escaped."

"Wasn't it any good? Who was there?"

"Elodie."

"That I know."

"And a rare animal from an endangered species."

"Listen, I'm kind of foggy. Talk normally, would you please? Who?"

"Me."

"Who else?"

"That was the entire guest list."

"What a nerve! And what did you do?"

"We made love!" He had no idea why this popped out of his mouth.

"I'm going to kill her! I'm going to kill her!"

"Shhhh!" whispered Dan.

"Uh!" said Jeremy.

"Watch!" said Benjamin.

"She planned it . . . an ambush!"

"You don't know the worst. She's taken your seat beside me at school."

"And you sat there and let her do it, Ernest Morlaisse?" Ernest didn't know what to say.

"I'll scratch her eyes out. Don't worry. She's not going to get away with it that easily!"

"It's no big deal. . . ."

"Ernest, I want you to know, I'm prepared to fight for you!"

"So am I, Victoria."

"They didn't name me Victoria for nothing."

"Shh! For once there's someone decent on TV."

Victoria lay down on the sofa. "Don't come too close," she told Ernest.

Monsieur de Montardent came in with a noisy "Hi everyone," then his wife, and a few more brothers, each with their own personal sound effects.

"Shhhhhh!"

Jeremy sought a different knee. He clambered onto Ernest and started tugging at his mask.

Dan stared at Ernest. "It's incredible how much he looks like you."

"Especially with the mask," said Ernest, thinking Dan meant he looked like the baby. But then Ernest studied the features of the man talking, and recognized himself. They had the same dimple in the chin, the same nose, the same mouth, the same eyes. Everybody has a similar set of features, but a millimeter can change Beauty into the Beast.

"This guy's gorgeous! He looks like a movie star!" cried Victoria.

Ernest always felt uneasy when people spoke of looks. "Gorgeous! There's more to life than looks, isn't there?" he said.

"It's still the first thing you notice!" Victoria retorted.

"Shh! It's the guy who wrote your book!"

Ernest stared at the screen and had to stop himself from going to touch the picture.

"Gaspard Morlaisse, have you managed to discover your father's secrets?" came the voice of the TV host.

"I never knew my father. He died on the front in 1940 before I was born."

"I never knew my father," thought Ernest. "And now I find we're in the same room. . . ."

"Is he related to you, Ernest?" asked Monsieur de Montardent.

Ernest replied, white as if he had seen a ghost. "He may just be my father."

And to himself he added, "I must be my father's secret."

In fact he knew it was his father. He knew this face by heart. It was the face on his grandmother's bedside table. "Is he really a father if he doesn't want to be a father?" whispered Ernest, almost inaudibly.

The interview finished, but Ernest stayed motionless. Perhaps, he thought, if he went on watching, the picture would come back. He was so caught up with longing and frustration that nothing could make him move

from his seat. In any case, Jeremy had planted himself
on his knee.

"So you know him?" asked Benjamin, immediately re-
gretting his question.

"He disappeared when I was born. Grandmother
never talks about him. There are a lot of secrets. I hate
them! Why can't we just talk about things? People
weren't put on earth to play hide-and-seek with them-
selves."

"That's a tough job," declared Madame de Montardent.

"Then what's the point?"

"Your father must have had a good reason."

"I was only one day old. What could I have done to
him?" Ernest fought back the tears which he felt
welling up in his eyes and irritating his nose.

Victoria moved her microbes next to him and
stroked his head.

"I never gave it much thought. I lived with Grandmother and I forced myself to believe that it was normal. It's only since I've been coming here that I've
realized what real families are like."

"But families also have their problems," interrupted
Madame de Montardent.

"So, we've gotten you upset. . . ." said Benjamin.

"Not at all. Because of you, I began asking Grandmother questions I had never even thought to ask. That's when she admitted that my father was alive. Then I came across his book. Then when we got our telephone, I looked him up in the phone book. Do you know that he lives in the same town as we do? Ever since I found out, I've been looking for him everywhere. I dream about him. And I really don't know what I could have done to make him abandon me forever."

"It must be something between him and your grandmother."

"Whatever it is, I am not even sure I would want a father who abandoned me like that."

"He must have had a reason."

"Maybe he was sick," added Issachar. "A manic depressive."

"Maybe he just completely forgot," suggested Benjamin.

Jeremy added an approving "Uh!"

Seeing how Ernest was feeling, Madame de Montardent declared, "Stay with us this evening."

"Thanks, but what about Grandmother?"

"We'll go and pick her up."

"You know she has her routine."

"From time to time you have to give routine a kick in the pants."

Dan got up with his car keys, but Issachar stopped him: "You know, I'm not sure it's such a good idea, having an old lady around with all these germs."

"No, really, I have to go. Thanks. Some other time," Ernest said.

Dan walked him to the door and whispered, "I put the address on your letter and mailed it."

Jeannette

Ernest was hardly expecting to find what he did when he got home. His grandmother was sitting on the sofa looking toward the sideboard, wide-eyed, with an expression of total distress on her face. He could barely believe what he saw next to the telephone, on the cabinet where the famous letter was buried—a tiny TV set. He raised his eyes to the ceiling to see if the TV had left a hole when it had dropped from the sky. The volume was deafening. Grandmother probably didn't realize that it could be turned down. "Where did this come from, Grandmother?" he asked, but the thunderstruck expression did not leave her face, and Ernest realized that she had seen the same ghost as him.

"You saw him too . . . you saw my father."

She bent her head and closed her eyes. You might have thought she was dead, except that the two slits under her forehead had brought forth two dewdrops which became torrents of tears. The gateway of the eyes is always open for tears.

Germs are contagious, and so are tears. Ernest flopped down beside his grandmother and sobbed as if he'd known how all his life. They stayed there crying long enough to water the dried-up plains of their hearts. Then Precious pulled herself together. "Jeannette and Henrietta brought the TV. They just bought a new one, and asked me if I could do them a favor and keep this one until Henrietta needs it."

"I saw him, Grandmother. I saw him on TV. Tell me what happened. Why did he leave us? What did you do to him?"

"I conceived him. I gave birth to him. I brought him up all alone. I loved him. I still do."

"Did you try to find him?"

"No. Motherhood does not last forever. There comes a day when children have to make their way."

"But he left me!"

Precious shrugged her shoulders and sighed.

"What happened, Grandmother?" Ernest repeated.

"I don't know. He couldn't face up to it. I didn't give him enough support. I don't know. . . ."

"He doesn't look like he's suffering."

"The worst pain you suffer alone. You can't tell how someone else suffers."

Ernest got up to turn off the crazed yelling of the TV. When it stopped, they both felt relieved.

"I've written to him, Grandmother."

Jeannette had taken to helping her daughter. Not that Henrietta didn't have enough energy, but Jeannette had grown attached to this odd family. She spent her day off keeping Precious company and giving her the latest gossip about the de Montardents. She loved them as if they were her own family, but she didn't always approve of their excessive exuberance, their excessive liveliness, and in general, their excessive numbers. "You realize, there are already sixteen of them. If each of them has a friend, it's an army. I'm not a camp director. Mind you, they do help me. They're good kids."

Jeannette went to pick up Germaine from the hospital and brought her back to the Morlaisses'. Three of the de Montardent boys had repainted one of the innumerable bedrooms to make her welcome. Germaine had gotten thinner and had become embittered. She immediately fell out of love with Jeannette and her daughter—that is, she fell into a general dislike which grew deeper with every new attack on her principles. According to Germaine, the meals were unhealthy and would be the death of Precious. That the old lady had put on weight, ate with a hunger that matched her new appetite for life, got dressed, made herself busy, and sometimes even laughed did not convince Germaine that her theories were mistaken. As for Ernest, she saw him turning bad by associating with all these oddballs.

She wanted to strangle Henrietta for doing everything that she had never thought of doing herself, and she would make a negative remark whenever she could. She would hide the spice jars and try to dampen her employer's enthusiasm by telling made-up tales about her replacement. She insisted that she was perfectly well enough to start working again, in order to get rid of the intruder.

"But you have three months sick leave. Take advantage of it, you deserve it."

On the other hand, Germaine worshipped the TV, which she watched from morning to night. She knew the schedule by heart and wouldn't miss her soaps for anything in the world. Everyone else was pleased, because the TV kept her quiet.

Ernest got sick soon after Victoria, with the same symptoms, which seemed to prove Germaine's theories about hanging around with oddballs. The only thing was, Germaine had a soft spot for Victoria. "She's a sensible one, that girl!" She was delighted when Victoria told them how she had managed to get her seat beside Ernest back. She had simply written this letter to the teacher:

Dear Sir,

As you know, I changed schools several times, until my parents finally found an apartment big enough for the sixteen of us. Little by little, I have begun to feel at home in your class, on the cozy little island I share with Ernest Morlaisse. He gives me lots of encouragement and help (you must have noticed my progress) and I will not hide from you the fact that we love each other and are going to get married (later).

There is no reason why Elodie Hainaut should take my seat. I know very well that

she is also in love with Monsieur Morlaisse.
But unfortunately, one doesn't always get
what one wants in life. However, I promise
you that if you don't give me my seat back, I
will fall apart. I can't even breathe anymore,
so you can imagine how that will affect my
work! (If you don't breathe, you can't work.)
I assure you, I am not just saying this. It is a
matter of life and death.

Here's hoping I can count on your good
judgment. I am sure that you will restore my
ideal pedagogical conditions.

> *Yours sincerely,*
> *Victoria*

Ernest was already flushed, but he got even redder when she read him the letter.

"Did you write this by yourself?"

"Yeah."

"Pedagogical?"

"Oh, that was Dan."

"I will fall apart?"

"That was Benjamin."

"Hoping I can count on your good judgment?"

"Simeon."

"And Jeremy?"

"Uh!"

"And Elodie?"

"Double uh! Double yuck! She doesn't speak to me anymore, and that's lucky, because I don't speak to her either."

"How nice!" Ernest chimed.

"Who?"

"You two!"

"You can't love everyone. We're already lucky to love the ones we love."

Although the house was never dull what with Germaine's jibes, Henrietta's high spirits, Precious's new outlook, and Ernest's expectations, the de Montardent brothers took turns coming by to keep him company anyway.

Ever since the telephone and the television had arrived on the dresser, Ernest had been thinking about the letter which had been so important in their other life. He decided to study it alone in his room, to have another try at decoding it. He was just looking over the hieroglyphics when Dan arrived. Seeing the letter he exclaimed, "You got a reply?"

Ernest raised his eyes sadly and explained, "No, this is

a letter my great-grandfather wrote from the front during the First World War, but we can't read it."

"You're joking! Let's see." Dan glanced at the letter and nodded. "There must be some kind of experts, graphologists, archivists, people they call paleographers, or even pharmacists who could decode this thing."

"Yes, but where do you get hold of them?"

"I'll find out," promised Dan. His place was immediately taken by Benjamin. Ernest still held the letter, with the envelope on his knees. Benjamin picked up the envelope, then put it down.

"That's really interesting!" he declared. "Can I borrow it?"

Ernest didn't like the idea of letting the letter out of the house.

"I just want to check something in my book."

"Couldn't you bring your book here?"

"Yes, if you like . . . good idea. I'll bring it next time. Are you feeling better?"

"I'll be okay," answered Ernest, thinking, "how okay *am* I going to be?"

Gaspard

Colds come and go. Although Ernest was not lazy, he enjoyed the feeling of being stuck in bed, drowned in blankets. Away from his bed there was a whole world, with people and things going on, but none of it had anything to do with him. Being sick is like taking a vacation from everyday life.

He went back to school, went back to Victoria, and went back to the world. He worked as he had before, he ate Henrietta's excellent cooking, listened to Germaine's sarcastic remarks, and he waited. He was expecting a letter. Days and weeks went by with no delivery. Then, one day, not a letter but a huge package

arrived on the doorstep, delivered by a red-faced, pant-
ing postman.

Gathering his strength, Ernest dragged the parcel
silently to his room without saying anything to the
women in the house. He untied the knots, unstuck
the sticky tape, opened the flaps, and lifted out ten
looseleaf notebooks. Each one was labeled with a year.
The first was the year he was born, then nine more, until this year. He opened the cover of the first one and
read:

> *My dear son,*
>
> *I have given you a name which is half
> mine and half yours, but I do not want to
> look after you. Your mother's burial was my
> burial, too. I am no longer a part of this
> world. Yes, I still breathe, I walk, I eat, I
> think, but I am somewhere else . . . with her.
> My pain is unbearable.*
>
> *Now that I've explained my feelings, I can
> tell you this: I am leaving you in my mother's
> care through pure selfishness. I can't deal
> with anyone besides myself. The truth is, I
> can no longer hold Colette in my arms.*

"But you still could have held me," thought Ernest, reading on. It was as if his correspondent had heard his question.

There you are, and I am your father. I always thought I was strong . . . until it was I who needed strength. The sad and somber life I lived with my mother prepared me well for studying, but not for life's realities. I'm running away, even though I realize that a person can never escape from himself. I have been offered a job in Canada. I'm going. I am an unforgivable coward. I don't know how I would be able to go on with my research with a baby to look after. Perhaps one day you will forgive me.

There was a letter for each day. His father had written to him every day of his life. Some letters were very long, describing his days in minute detail, others were philosophical, others about his historical research. Each letter began with "My dear son." Ernest read a few weeks' correspondence at a time.

It was hard for him to pace his reading, because he wanted to take it all in at once. Each letter gave him a little bit more of his father, and he felt himself swelling inside until he thought his heart would burst.

He spent so much time with his father that even when he wasn't in his room reading, he had no time for Victoria. His gaze was far away and impenetrable. Victoria kept her distance—she was sensitive enough to realize that he didn't want to be disturbed. Germaine put his silence down to the fact that he had become "normal" again. Henrietta lectured him while stuffing him with her latest culinary exploits, and his grandmother quietly wondered what was going on. He didn't tell them about his letters.

Only Benjamin came to see him regularly, with various books about stamp collecting. Ernest thought regretfully of the number of stamps he could have given to his friend if his father had sent all those letters in the mail.

The letters followed Gaspard's travels from university to university, across Canada and the United States until he finally settled in Cambridge, Massachusetts, where he met Jennifer, an American linguist, and remarried.

He wrote, "The emptiness in my heart is too deep to be filled, but this new love is soothing to the wound."

According to Ernest's father, this young American woman spoke good French. One day she announced that she was pregnant. Over the next six years, she was to make this announcement three more times. Thus Ernest discovered that he was the eldest of a huge family, with four sisters named Myrtle, Clementine, Cherry, and Peach. Their ages were respectively six, four, two, and six months. Ernest thought that the baby should marry Jeremy. Every time he thought about them, he was seized by a longing to meet them that was more than a mere wish or hope. He even started to eat chocolate in order to calm this burning desire. His father assured him that the new members of the family had in no way taken his place, and that he would always be Gaspard's eldest and only son. He read over these missing links to his life story until the early hours of the morning. Never again would he come across such fascinating reading. He didn't want to reach the end, but couldn't stop himself from devouring page after page.

He got to the time when his father took up a year-long job in France.

It was to get closer to you, to try to get in touch. I waited for you outside school, the same school I went to myself, but I never managed to talk to you. What was I going to say? "Hiya buddy. I'm your father. Don't you remember me? I'm the guy who abandoned you when you were one day old, and condemned you to the same ghastly existence I had lived myself." Then I realized that I had turned you into my twin. I'm not quite sure if all fathers do this. The longer I waited, the more difficult it became to introduce myself. It became an impossibility. I have behaved monstrously. And I know, too, that recognizing one's mistakes does not erase them.

I hung around near the house. I saw this pretty little friend make her way into your life and bring a smile to your face. I even saw what I would have thought impossible: I saw my mother and you going out together one sunny Sunday.n

My poor mother. What can I say? She did her pathetic best. She has been traumatized her whole life. Some people can get over hard times. She is not one of them. In my own cowardly and treacherous way, even I got over them. If I betrayed you, Ernest, I never really left you. You have always been with me. As

126

for my mother, she did what she could for you, just as she did for me.

My Ernest, to get closer to you I went to talk to your teacher. He told me that students like you only come along for a teacher once in a lifetime. It made me proud, even though I had never done anything to help you. He said that your schoolwork was so strong, so far beyond what he expected, that he never thought twice about the rest of your life until the day you wrote an essay about a Sunday with my mother.

Ernest, I wanted you, and then I no longer wanted you, but I haven't spent an instant of my life without you. I have written to you every day, but more for myself than for you. I've thought of you from morning to night. I know, it hasn't been a lot of use to you. I don't know if you can forgive me. I do know that I can't forgive myself. I have deprived myself of watching you grow up, perhaps to punish myself for your mother's death. She wanted you too. She was the victim of a stupid accident (Is there such a thing as an accident which isn't stupid?): uncontrollable hemorrhaging. She was an orphan herself—

a woman who lived calmly. I loved her so
completely. I became crazed by this love—
especially once I could no longer have her.

Now I think I have gotten over it. Not ex-
actly over it, but at least now I can function.
Now I want to hold you in my arms and talk
to you face to face. I want to see you every
day. I want you to meet your sisters and my
wife, who I only told about you recently. That
was my secret.

I'd like to think that wanting things to
happen makes them come true. As if one
could have anything merely by wanting it.
As you can imagine, money has always been
tight—teaching doesn't exactly pay a for-
tune.

Ernest, I am your father, a disappointing
and powerless father who thinks that think-
ing is enough and that the thought counts
more than the deed.

The last letter was dated the day before the package arrived and was in response to Ernest's letter.

Ernest, my dear Ernest, you have an-
swered all my prayers. You are the one with

the courage I never had. You are the one who
found me. It's our children who teach us
how to be parents. I've waited too long.
Come see me as soon as you can. We'll be go-
ing back to the U.S.A. in just a few weeks.

Ernest was furious with himself for not having read the last letter first. Maybe it was already too late.

Adrian

By the time Ernest had reached the end of his ten volumes of letters, winter was long gone, taking with it its flu and misery. The spring was well on its way to summer, and the sunshine lingered for three minutes longer each day. Henrietta hummed into her sauces, Germaine muttered in front of the TV, and Precious bided her time. One day, Victoria knocked at the door with Jeremy in her arms. She announced, "Look and you shall see what you shall see!" She put Jeremy down, and he staggered like a drunkard toward Germaine, who commented, "That brings back memories. . . ."

With a decided air, Ernest slipped into the living

room that had been cleared of its usual TV viewers. He dialed his father's phone number. He had already practiced this move a hundred times before, but he still hadn't done it for real.

School wound its way down to the end of the year. Ernest would often go to the de Montardents after class. He liked to watch Jeremy's staggering progress. He would take him to the park and have fun chasing after him. "It's unbelievable!" Ernest would cry.

"We've all been through it," Victoria would say.

One Wednesday morning, Ernest felt ready for the visit. That's the way it is—you have a thought, a dream, an idea in your head . . . and you do nothing to make it happen. Then one day, boom, just like that, you get up and go.

Ernest set himself in motion—he got a map, put his finger on the right street, guessed the way, and arrived there with no problem. He rang the bell of the building and got the same reply as he had on the phone. No one home.

He asked the doorman, who told him that the Morlaisses had left for America the previous week. "I certainly miss those kids. They're so cute!"

Ernest left, then returned to the doorman, asking, "Did they leave an address?"

"Yes, hold on, I'll give it to you."

Ernest felt like a cherry tree cut down just when the fruit was ripe. Amputated! He retraced his steps, as wobbly on his legs as Jeremy. He made up a letter in his head: "Dear Father, I already forgave you once. I read all your letters, which fed me crumbs of love and admiration. Like Hansel and Gretel, I followed their trail to your door. But you have left me again. I have the whole summer ahead of me to re-read your letters, and to try to understand."

He took the letter to the post office, where for the first time he saw beautiful stamps on display. He joined the line, and paid with the money he had borrowed from Henrietta.

He waited through the June heat, but he didn't have to wait long before getting a reply. He received a new package of letters, the last of which invited him to spend his summer vacation in the U.S. "If my mother agrees, I'd like her to come with you. I'd like her to meet her granddaughters, and I'd like to tell her I'm sorry and that I love her. I'll find a way to send you the tickets. If you want my mother to read the letters, go ahead and let her."

Ernest's heart thumped hard against his chest. He paced around the apartment six times, like a gorilla in a cage. He really wanted to show the letters to his grandmother, even if he had to take out those which described her as doing her "pathetic best." He dragged the edited version of the carton into Precious's room. "My father wrote me a letter a day from the day I was born. I got them a few months ago. I'd be happy if you read them, Grandmother."

He would tell her later about the invitation to America, but he told Victoria right away.

"You lucky thing! It's what I've always dreamed of."

"Maybe you could come with us, although I'm sure that Grandmother isn't going to want to go."

The whole de Montardent family was delighted about the coming reunion between Ernest and his father, and his new family. Ernest would have liked to share the letters with them, too.

Dan had good news for Ernest. "I spoke to one of the professors who's really big in paleography. He'd be glad to take a look at your mysterious letter."

The coming and going between the two houses had become so frequent that Ernest got the letter to Dan in no time. "I'm sure I don't need to tell you to guard it with your life. I didn't mention it to Grandmother."

"Want to come with me?" asked Dan.

"Yes, I'd love to. I've been trying for so long to make sense of this letter."

"Okay. I'll make an appointment for next Wednesday after my exams."

Precious only left her room at mealtimes, and when she did appear, it was often with red, swollen eyes. Germaine was preparing to go back to her own home. Now she was back on her feet, she felt as if she would drown in Henrietta's rich, creamy cooking. In fact, Henrietta had been offered a job on the French Riviera, cooking in a small hotel for the summer season. Precious encouraged her to accept. "We'll manage."

Ernest felt that this was the right moment to bring up his father's invitation, but he still didn't dare.

He finished the school year in his usual glorious position of number one. The principal even kissed him when she presented him with his prize—the complete works of Shakespeare, which he had already gotten the year before. Victoria was complimented for having made such good progress, and Ernest rewarded her with the Shakespeare.

Victoria went with him and Dan to see the paleographer, who actually managed to decode the ancient letter. Ernest took down the words as the expert deciphered them. The result was this:

My dear family,
    It is very cold here on the front. Could you send me some warm underwear and socks? Thank you for the cake and the trousers.
                Affectionately,
                Adrian

Ernest felt odd, stupid, disappointed, and surprised. "Is that all?"

"That's all."

"Are you positive?"

"I'm afraid so. This is a typical letter from a soldier to his family, a soldier who is cold and scared, and who doesn't want to say any more."

"Should we tell Grandmother?" Ernest asked Dan.

"She might be relieved. One more mystery cleared up. One less secret."

"We'll come with you," said Victoria.

They found Precious engrossed in conversation with Benjamin, who jumped when he saw them.

"Grandmother, I've got something to tell you. Dan helped me. I took the letter to a professor and he decoded it. This is what it said." He handed her the paper, and instead of crying, his grandmother burst out laughing.

"But that's a fantastic secret, Ernest. That is the secret of life: try to survive! This calls for celebration. Henrietta has prepared a going-away party, and *all* the de Montardents are invited."

"But I expected that letter to be much more exciting!" exclaimed Ernest.

"Tell him, Benjamin," said Precious encouragingly.

"The letter might not be what you expected, but the stamp is worth a fortune! It's one of a common series of the time, but it has an imperfection. I've found a dealer who is willing to pay a fabulous price."

"You're not serious?"

"Yes I am."

Henrietta came in carrying a chocolate mousse and a large envelope. "Your tickets have arrived, Ernest."

"Will you come, Grandmother?"

"Of course, Ernest. Those tickets won't be any good when we're both dead."

Ernest sat down with his forehead behind his arms to hide his tears. Nobody bothered him.

When he raised his eyes, he saw Victoria, and a drop of sadness trickled into his river of happiness. "I won't see you for the whole summer."

"Ernest," said his grandmother, "there are three tickets, and one of them is in the name of Mademoiselle Victoria de Montardent. Your father spoke with her parents."

Victoria bounded over to Ernest, kissing Precious, Henrietta, her brothers, and the sky. "It's our advance honeymoon!"

And Benjamin gave out a yell, just like one of the early American pioneers: "Westward ho!"